CW00972043

The Hunter: Trials and Revelations

This is a work of fiction. Any similarities to persons living or dead is unintentional and purely coincidental. Also, and mistakes or faults are mine alone.

Front cover image by Very Metal Art www.verymetal.co.uk

For the latest updates search James Manning Author on Facebook

Books by James Manning

Between A Rock And A Bad Place

I.R.I.S.

Deliver Us From Evil

Books in the Chris Spencer series

The Hunter: The Hunted And The Prey

The Hunter: Subversion

The Hunter: Trials and Revelations

For my readers.

The Allosaurus bellowed, the heavy sound rolling like thunder. It faced the small man with almost drooling anticipation. The man snarled defiance, then ran at the beast. The Allo lowered its head, ready for its meal to run into its mouth. The man ran to the rows of teeth, then ducked. In a blur he was airborne, flipping over the flat snout and landing on the wide head. Sliding a blade from his belt the man kept his footing as the head rose. The Allo tried to shake him free, but the man slid in a controlled glide down the thick neck. The blade flashed in the midsummer light and the man rolled as he plunged the blade into the back of the head.

The Allo gave a surprised cough, then dropped slowly to the floor. The man rode it down, rolling off the head and finishing on one knee before the watching villagers. He rose to cheers. Waving a hand the man accepted the applause and walked back to his cart. Today was a good day to be him. He was Greg 'Flair' Numlok, and he was a Hunter.

Chapter 1

"Bloody stupid thing," Chris moaned softly. The rifle in his hands clicked gently as he eased the safety catch free. His prey heard the noise, the small head twitching as it looked around. Cursing under his breath Chris rose from the bush he was hiding in and aimed. The rifle kicked once, and the sheep fell dead.

"What happened to being quiet?" a nearby bush asked.

"Bloody safety stuck," Chris said, showing the rifle.

The bush shook. "Need to take care of your weapon better," it said.

Chris gave the bush a kick. "I'm the one who tells you that."

"True," said Marty, stepping out of his bush. He rubbed his hip where Chris had kicked him.

"Well, we better hope one sheep is enough to last us," Chris said, watching the rest of the flock running over the hill.

"We have plenty back home," Marty said, kneeling beside the sheep, drawing his knife to butcher it.

"True, but that ain't gonna last forever."

Chris left Marty to gut the sheep while he got the car. Since the world had fallen food was scarce, and most villages survived only on what they grew. If the crops failed, the people starved. Animals were rare in the wilderness, and these sheep had been a blessing. The two men should have caught them easily, but the lapse in concentration on Chris' part had let them escape. For most it was an irritation, for a seasoned Hunter like Chris it was inexcusable.

Pulling the branches off his car Chris half smiled at the familiar boxy shape. The car, like his rifle, was even more unusual in these times. Most people used stones, sharpened sticks, or scavenged blades. Chris had weapons that fired metal slugs, bombs and explosives. He found a military bunker early on in his career as a Hunter, and that gave him the edge. Marty argued Chris was the best Hunter alive. Chris was just happy to be alive.

They were three days into stalking a small carnivore. Usually Deinonychus hunted in packs, but this one must have been an outcast. A village had lost some people to it, so they called for Chris. Luckily for them he was nearby, and the small boy who had run for miles to find him was glad of a ride in the magical cart. The old Land Rover was a remnant of the past, the time before now, where they had a civilisation that flew to the stars, could talk to each other when they were miles apart, and lived in big houses. Now most lived in mud huts, except those in the big cities. Chris avoided the cities, after two separate occasions where he'd tried to help them and been double-crossed. Now he only wanted to be out in the wild.

A low whistle instantly put him on guard. He lifted his rifle and stalked through the long grass and stumpy bushes. Marty was waiting, and pointed at their sheep. He had backed away when he first heard the noise of the dinosaur, and let it scavenge off their kill. Chris cursed his failing hearing.

With only eye contact, Chris told Marty to move to one side. With weapons ready they got the Deiny in a cross fire. It tried to run, but the hail of bullets cut out it's legs and it fell. Chris took his pistol while Marty reloaded his rifle. Aiming the small gun at the writhing head Chris pulled the trigger. The head lay still.

"A decent result, I guess," Marty said, looking at the remains of their sheep.

"Any kill is a win for us." Chris knelt down and used his knife to sever the head. Tucking it under his arm he walked back to the car. Marty followed.

"We going back tonight?" Marty asked.

Chris slung the head into the back of the car.. "Not tonight," he replied, looking at the sky. "Be dark by the time we get half way there."

"So where we sleeping?"

"Best do it in the open."

"More night watches?" Marty asked with a deeply unhappy tone.

"Yeah, more night watches. Can't have anything sneak up on us."

"You could set traps?"

Chris slid into the worn driver's seat and waited for Marty to get into the passenger side. "We can't sleep when we are out in the open. You know that. A wild dog could sneak past a mile of traps and have an arm off you before you even knew it."

"I know, just hate night work."

"Hey, we're getting paid. We did good." Chris started the old diesel and they rocked away.

Chapter 2

Greg held his hands high as he entered the village. The crowds mobbed him, but he liked it that way. Hands touched him with gentle reverence as the elder hobbled over to thank him.

"We are blessed by you, oh Hunter," the elder said, clasping one of Greg's hands in his. "Truly blessed."

"Indeed you are," Greg replied. "And you can sleep well tonight, all of you." He pulled his hands free and waved them over the crowd, who cheered. In the gateway to the mud village the cart carrying the severed head creaked as two men pulled it. Both were fairly tall for the wilderness, but where one was stocky like Greg, the other was thin and weedy. They struggled with the cart, the mid year heat making the ground like stone, and the cart felt like it was stone too.

"He killed it, he should move it," the weedy man said, leaning on one of the shafts.

"He killed it because he's good," the other replied with undisguised aggression. "We work with him, so we help by bringing the kill back. Quit your complaining. We're there nearly."

The weedy man sneered, but lifted his side and they dragged the head inside the mud walls. The gate closed behind them, and Greg came and stood on one of the shafts, placing a hand on the head. He faced the crowd, speaking loudly so they could all hear.

"This monster stole your flocks, your livelihood, and even your families. Now you have stolen it's head. There are many dangers out there, but there is always me, who will protect you from them."

"Except when we ain't here," the weedy man said.

Greg shot him a look, then resumed. "You only need call, and we will come running to help our friends here. I always have time for this village." The crowds cheered again, and Greg dropped from the cart, scooping several young women in his arms and leading them to a mud hut. The two men watched him go.

"He always gets the best of the women too," the weedy man said.

"Listen, Jake, you gotta bide your time, and hold hard to Greg. He's good, you can learn a lot."

"I know, but it winds me up something chronic that he gets all the rewards."

"He deserves it. You can be Greg, one day, maybe."

"Yeah right. What about you, Ben? When you gonna be Greg?"

Ben leant on the cart and looked at the mud hut. He was built like Greg, only slightly slimmer. He had known Greg all his life, both of them growing up in a farming city. When some wild dogs broke in through the gate and killed some of the cattle, Greg went on the warpath, killing them all and hanging their tails around his neck. Ben Jackson had helped, and the credit was shared, more towards Greg, but shared. He knew all the tricks, but let his better take the credit, and the risk.

Jake Smith was a farmhand from one of the farms. He had helped round up the dogs, and even knocked one down with a club. It was attacking Greg, who was gracious of the help. When the pack was destroyed Greg found he liked the attention, so went hunting. Jake and Ben followed, equally attracted to the spoils of success.

"I may be Greg one day," Ben admitted. "But not for a while. He needs our help."

"True. Just wish he thought about us over himself occasionally."

"He does," Ben said.

"When?"

"You're still here, ain't you?" Ben wandered over to the communal pot and scooped some stew into an earthen bowl. Jake watched, then joined him. The screams from the mud hut showed Greg was enjoying himself. The others knew their payment would come tomorrow, with every piece of shiny jewellery this village could find.

Chapter 3

In the early morning Marty woke in his green sleeping bag to see his breath fog before his face. It was cold, and the first rays of the sun were bright beams aimed into his mind. He tried hiding his head in the hood of his sleeping bag, but he was awake, and the professional side of him was on alert.

"About time you woke up," Chris said. He was standing on the flat bonnet of the car, using far seers to look around them.

"How did you know I was awake?" Marty asked, wriggling out of the bag.

"The ground stopped shaking with your snores."

"Sod off," Marty said, falling out of his hammock and landing on the ground with a thud. "You snore louder than me."

"If you made any more noise in bed I'd have to bury you ten feet under to keep us hidden from a deaf old woman, and even then she might hear you."

"You're still louder," Marty replied, shaking the dirt off his sleeping bag and rolling it up.

"But I do it at the right pitch to keep everything away from us." Chris smiled as he scanned the terrain.

"What pitch? Loud?"

"Exactly. Now you're up you can get brekkie on the go."

"Why don't you?"

Chris waved the black far seers, then resumed looking through them. "I'm working."

"Looks like you're working too hard. You need a rest."

"We all do, but you ain't gonna get out of cooking so get the hexy-stove out."

Marty threw his sleeping bag into a metal locker box and rummaged for the small metal solid fuel stove, muttering to himself.

"I ain't old, or deaf either," Chris said.

Marty looked up in surprise, then smiled. Chris was older than most people Marty met on their travels, but his physical condition was that of a man half his age. Neither of them knew their exact age, but they could compare to others. The silver hair that flecked Chris' head was slowly taking over, and only a few hobbling elders lived to have much more white hair than Chris had now.

"What you wanting then?" Marty asked, opening the metal stove that was the size of his fist and lighting the white block of fuel with a match.

"Got any of that syrup pudding left?"

"For breakfast?"

Chris dropped down from the bonnet, wincing as his right knee buckled. "Why not? It's good enough for evening, so why not for breakfast?"

"It's so thick and sweet."

"Like me, then."

"Well, the thick part maybe," Marty said, already ducking the hand that was aimed for the back of his head.

"I'm sweet enough perhaps. How about some stew?"

Marty waved a silver foil pouch. "Last one."

"Really? We had loads of 'em."

"You ate loads of them," Marty replied. "Only got the sausage casserole, or the curry if you fancy that."

"That's too much for brekkie. I'll have the sausage I think."

Marty dropped two pouches into a metal tin and filled it with water from a bottle. Resting the tin on the prongs of the stove he waited for the water to boil. Chris took a folding shovel and wandered off, but not too far.

Chris stood and wiggled his legs. "That's better. You really should settle down sometime, boy."

"You didn't."

"I did, once." Chris squatted beside Marty, hooking a pouch with his fingertips.

"I know, and that's why I don't wanna settle."

"Not everyone gets killed by raiders, you know?"

Marty took his own pouch and laid it on the ground to cool a little. They both wetted their faces and used the hot water to shave.

"I know that," he said when he had finished, handing the razor to Chris. "It's just, being in one place, means I'm chained there. I like to be able to move."

"I know the feeling," Chris said, pulling a funny face while he shaved. "This life can be lonely, but at least you know you are free."

"Free and wild," Marty said, rubbing his smooth chin.

"And hungry," Chris said, rinsing the razor in the hot water before opening his pouch. He smelt the steaming contents. "You know, this could be worse?"

"How?"

"Could be cold and wet."

Marty looked at the clear sky. It would be another hot day. The farmers would be checking the water for their cattle, and making sure their crops were watered. The sun soon would be high, trying to burn the surface away.

"Cold ain't gonna be a problem for a while," Marty said.

"True. But dust will. Best get the big gun stripped and oiled, then check the ammo links. Don't want it jamming and we've been neglecting it awhile."

Marty pulled a face, but nodded. It was a pain stripping the heavy gun mounted on the top of the car, but both of them knew it could mean the difference between life and death.

They spent the morning well, using the post dawn coolness to strip and clean all their weapons, and repacking the back of the Land Rover. By the time the sun was really making an effort to be uncomfortable they were ready and heading out. Chris drove them down from the plateau they had slept on and back towards the village that had hired them. They needed the cured meat they would be paid in, and the chance to refill their water from the village well was a welcome opportunity. Living in the wilds always came with the risk of running out of the basics, and Chris took great care checking everything.

Chapter 4

They arrived at the village as the sun reached it's most intense. Marty missed the cool breeze in his face from the drive. The heat enveloped them as soon as they stopped, but Chris ignored it. Taking the head from the back of the car he presented it to the village elder.

"Many thanks, Hunter," the old man said, bowing before he waved two men to take the head away. "You have avenged our losses. We can move on now in our lives."

"Anything to help, we will do. Just call."

"If we can find you, Hunter. Our threats are many, and Hunters are few. If you could stay amongst us, we could be assured of safety."

Chris smiled. He'd had this offer countless times before. "I wish I could, but then what would happen to the other villages? I'm needed all over, just as you said. Need to keep moving. Sorry."

"I understand. Thank you once again." The elder hobbled away, two young men supporting him. Chris wondered how long the old man had left, but that led him to wonder how long he himself would live, so he thought on his next job instead.

Marty was hanging some of their payment from the metal cage that protected the car if it rolled over. Four joints of what looked like smoked goat were hung from wooden pegs. It took some securing, but Marty managed to tie them on while the young women watched. Recently Marty had taken to wearing the green short sleeved cloth tops from the back of the bunker, enjoying the softer material, and the chance to reveal the strong arms he had been working on in the gym back home. Chris used the equipment to maintain his overall health, but Marty had been lifting the metal weights instead. He looked quite strong now. Some of the young girls called him a god on the ground with his muscular physique. They tended to be difficult to remove from Marty once they got a hold of him.

"We loaded?" Chris asked.

"Pretty much," Marty said, purposefully flexing his arms, enjoying the reactions from the women.

"Good. Gotta go."

Marty looked ready to cry. "What? Why?"

"We got work to do."

Marty was about to protest when a young man came over. By the cut of his animal skins he was attached to the village elder somehow. He held out a hand and waited. Chris paused, then shook the man's hand.

"Thank you, Hunter, from all of us," the man said.

"You're welcome. Anything we can do to help."

"You have made a big difference in this village. You seem to have the reputation for that."

"That's only gossip," Chris said.

"True," the man agreed. "So, you'll be doing the Trials then?"

"Trials?"

"The Hunter Trials. One of the big cities is searching for the best Hunter. If you win then you won't be gossip. You will be known as the best Hunter all over the plains."

Chris smiled. "I don't need a title. I do a job. That's enough for me."

"Think it over, Hunter. I would be proud to be helped by the best Hunter."

"I will," Chris said. The man shook his hand again, bowed briefly to Marty, then left.

"We doing it then?" Marty asked.

Chris got into the driver's seat. "Get in and shut up."

"What?" Marty slid into his seat, checking the small machine gun mounted on the dashboard before him.

"We ain't going to any more cities."

"Why not?"

Chris drove them out of the village gate, waving to the people who followed. When they were clear he spoke. "Remember what happens every time we go into a city?"

"Well, that may not happen again. Third time lucky, eh?"

"Lucky for them, or us?"

Marty hissed. "I doubt they would even be able to get at us. If there's loads of us out there they can't take on one single person."

"They'll find a way. I'm happy being known as me. I don't need any titles."

"What about the money? We could charge extra if we had a win under our belts."

"We charge what we need, not what we want. There's a difference. Our services for food. What we gonna do with money out here?"

Marty looked around at the empty plains.

"We could build a house."

Chris looked at him, then back to the dirt track. "You serious? Build a house? Why?"

"Somewhere to live."

"We have somewhere to live."

"Yeah. A hole in the ground."

"It's better than most have."

Marty was about to speak, but Chris held up a hand, silencing him.

"Did you see something?" Marty asked softly.

"Nope. Just wanted you to shut up a while."

Marty slipped into a moody silence, leaving Chris to wander with his mind and body over the plains.

"Bet we don't have a job either," Marty said after a while.

"Nope," Chris said, almost happily.

"Well that sucks even more."

"Saved you some energy. You can sleep tonight."

"Rather not sleep with them girls."

"In that case I saved them some sleep," Chris said.

"I never sleep with you around, snoring like a dino."

"That's what keeps them away at nights," Chris said with pride.

"And everyone else."

"Suits me. Bit of peace and quiet."

"Peace and quiet? You snore loud enough to wake the dead."

Chris clipped him with the back of his hand gently. "You just snore like the dead. I need to keep you on your toes."

"By keeping me awake?"

"You're welcome to sleep someplace else."

"No thanks. I'd rather have no sleep over being eaten by something."

"So stop your whining and sleep now if you're tired. We've gotta head back home. Need to replen."

"Can't sleep with your driving either."

Chris smiled and jiggled the steering wheel. "What a shame for you."

Chapter 5

They drove on in silence, both automatically scanning the landscape for threats. Marty saw something small in the distance, and waved to Chris.

"What's that, to our half left?" he asked.

"Where?" Chris replied, knowing his eyesight was growing steadily worse.

"There, between that stumpy bush and the leaning tree."

Chris slowed down, looking all around, then trying to follow Marty's pointing finger.

"What leaning tree?"

Marty dropped his hand. "Seriously? You can't see the tree?"

"Not that far away. Get me a lens."

Marty chuckled and climbed into the back. Taking a far seer he handed it to Chris. Peering through the black tubes Chris pursed his lips.

"Looks like a kid. He's running from something, or to something." He handed the far seers to Marty.

"We gonna help him?" Marty asked, focusing on the kid.

"Would be rude not to. I wanna know why he's out here alone."

Chris sped up, making it harder for Marty to keep his sight on the child. When they drew close the kid looked exhausted. He was covered in dirt, sweating badly in the midday heat, and panting. Chris stopped the car and got out slowly. The kid saw him and slowed down, unsure if he should go to Chris, or run from him.

"Easy, kiddo," Chris said, arms out wide. "We ain't gonna hurt you. Just wonderin' why you're out here alone."

The kid slowed to a walk but didn't change from his path. He looked at the car, and Marty, then back to Chris.

"You Hunter?" the kid asked.

"Yeah, I'm a Hunter," Chris said.

"You hunt things?" The kid stood still, the innocence of a child on his face.

"I hunt things." Chris kept his voice soft and friendly.

"I was told to go to other village, to get help."

"What is the problem?"

The kid looked at Marty, who winked. He looked over his shoulder, uncertain.

"Wassup, kid?" Chris asked again.

"There is something back home. Took some sheepies." The kid was trying to sound brave, but small tears formed in his eyes. "And my brother."

"Some sheepies and your brother," Chris repeated. "What kind of things?"

"Small hairy things, like sheepies with hair."

Chris looked at Marty. "Dogs, I think."

Marty nodded. "Don't worry, kid. We have taken care of more dog packs than you have had warm milk."

The kid smiled. "You find hairy sheepies?"

"We find 'em," Chris said. His heart went out to this kid. He could only be a few seasons old. It was a mystery why a village would send such a young boy to get help, but the only way to find out was to go.

Marty helped the kid into the back, giving him a black plastic water bottle, while Chris drove. They kept asking for directions, and the small boy tried to help them, but it was getting late by the time they found the village. Driving up to the still open gates Chris let the boy go in first while they waited to be invited inside. The village elder came out, more sprightly than most these days.

"Greetings, Hunter," the elder said, shaking hands. To Marty he looked nearly the same age as Chris.

"Greetings elder, and thank you for allowing us to enter your village," Chris said.

"Always space for a Hunter inside our walls. I hear you found poor Jacob in the wilds?"

"The boy? Yes, we found him. He said you had a dog pack problem."

The elder nodded, his face darkening. "They come at night. No idea where from, but we have lost several of our flock, and some of our men too. Jacob's older brother, Carl, went out with their father to find the pack. Only the father returned. He's with our healer now."

"We can deal with this for you," Chris said.

"You have our gratitude, Hunter," the elder said.

Once a price was agreed, and a place to sleep organised, Chris went back to the Land Rover.

"We sleeping here?" Marty asked.

"Yep." Chris put the car into gear and drove around the small mud huts to the wall opposite the gates. Then he checked the walls inside and out, walking the small step built into the top of the wall as well. He visited the elder, making suggestions about improving the walls' strength, before joining Marty, who was checking the car over.

"Oil's getting a bit low," Marty said, looking at the dipstick.

"Get some out the back then," Chris replied, stringing his hammock to a small tree.

"If we have any."

"Why we were going to restock after we sort this dog pack."

Marty rummaged in the maintenance box until he found a can of oil. Topping up the engine levels he looked at the villagers. They were all sitting on the dirt floor around the communal fire. The womenfolk were serving their families from a large pot that sat in the fire. The boy they had found clung to a man who was presumably his father, healing poultices on his arms and face showed the fight with the dogs.

"You noticed we seem to have more things to deal with these days?" Marty asked.

"I had," Chris said, tying the other end of his hammock to the back of the car.

"Wonder why."

"Weather, food, seasons, load of explanations."

Marty dropped the flat bonnet, apologising for making the whole village jump from the bang. "What do you think is causing it?"

"There are more people. More people make more food, and live in more places. Those big cities are expanding again. That pushed the wild animals out."

"What about the dinos? They ain't exactly a dog pack."

"True," Chris said. "I'm not sure that lab I found was the only one."

"Or they were made to survive longer?"

"Possible. Anyway, let's get some food on the go."

Marty coughed. "I don't think we need worry about getting food."

Chris looked up from his hammock to see a young girl bring two bowls of stew over.

"The elder offers this food to you, Hunter, and invites you to our fire," she said, staring at the floor.

"We are honoured to join you," Chris said, taking a bowl. Marty took the other and they followed the girl back to the ring of people.

Sitting down they shared stories, songs and more food. Marty had the unattached females watching him as usual, and he waited impatiently for a chance to dive out of the circle to join them. When the families went to bed, Chris sat with the elder and the older men of the village while Marty made his excuses and went back to the car. Chris knew Marty wouldn't be there when he went to bed, but the boy was a man now, and could make his own choices. Ignoring the dangers of the world outside the walls, Chris listened to the tales from the villagers and relaxed, keeping one hand by his pistol, just in case.

Chapter 6

The morning dew was fading when the gates opened. Chris went out first, rifle raised. Marty followed, also on alert. They scanned the ground outside the gates, then around the walls. The scanty crops growing beyond the high mud walls were undisturbed, and there was no sign of anything, human or animal, having been active in the night.

Satisfied, Chris went back inside. He drove the car out, Marty jumped on as he passed. They headed for the last known place the boy's brother had been seen. Marty slid into the driver's seat when they got there, Chris already searching for tracks. He walked in a random pattern, bent double. Marty knelt on the flat bonnet and held his rifle to his shoulder, only half watching Chris.

"Over here," Chris said. "Bloody big pack too by the sign."

Marty stayed where he was, but glanced in Chris' direction. "How big is 'big' ?"

"Big enough to give us some aggro. Best find them, then decide what we do. Get the extra mags ready, and be sure everything is fully loaded. We may need all the rounds we have for this."

Marty nodded and dropped to the floor. He started with the small machine gun mounted on the dash, lifting the lid on the metal ammunition box and checking the links. Then he checked the big gun mounted on the top of the roll cage, the metal box was bigger, but the same design. Inside the thumb sized rounds slept in their copper blankets, waiting. The metal storage bins in the back held everything they carried, and Marty checked the lot, ensuring what should move did, and what shouldn't move stayed still. Chris kept checking the trail, trying to count the dogs in this pack.

"Still say they could be good pets," Marty said.

"Dogs are vicious animals. You can't tame them."

"Think of how good they would be as a guard for us."

"Rip your throat out while you slept. Nice." Chris checked his rifle, working the bolt, listening to the sounds it made.

"If you found a young one you could tame it?"

"Look, let's just do this. If we find any young ones then we can see."

Marty creased his brows. "What's got into you?"

"Nothing, I just don't like being out here with a hundred dogs wandering around."

"There's that many?"

Chris pulled an exasperated face. "No, there ain't. I was exaggerating." He sighed. "Let's just do this. I feel for these things. Maybe they were pets once. I think I saw a pic of one with a person in the lab. Maybe not. Right now it's a threat, so let's neutralise it."

"Right. Let's go." Marty got into the passenger seat.

"What you doing?" Chris asked. He hadn't moved.

"Getting ready to go."

"You drive. I need to track 'em." Chris sat on the flat bonnet, feet resting on the square radiator grille. "And go steady. Don't be firing me off this thing."

"Why not?" Marty asked with a hint of humour.

"Because I'll have to break your jaw and that leaves me with nobody to talk to."

Marty started the diesel engine and manhandled the gear lever into first gear. "You say I talk too much."

"True. May do it anyway."

"How do I eat?" Marty asked as he pulled away gently.

Chris bent over the front, holding onto the clips that held the bonnet down to stop himself falling off. "I'll feed you."

"Can't chew with a broken jaw."

"I can mash it up for you. Maybe I could chew it for you."

"Think I'd rather starve."

"Shame. Well, more food for me."

"And less sleep," Marty pointed out.

"Without you I'd get more sleep. Left a little, please."

Marty turned the big wheel to his right.

"Left, you little git," Chris said.

"I did."

"My left, not yours."

Marty turned left. "What's the difference?"

"My left is the same as everyone else's."

Marty looked at his hands as the car rolled slowly over the trampled grass and bare earth. The sun beat down already, cooking them. Chris felt the heat from the tired engine through his bum, the unhappy rattle of the old diesel was concerning. There was only a certain number of times he could rebuild the car. There were spares in the hanger. Maybe there was another engine too.

Guided by the head gestures from Chris they stopped by a thick copse of trees. The brown grass was flat here from a lot of small feet. Chris slid from the bonnet, motioning Marty to turn the car around. With his rifle in his hands, Chris crept forwards, using the trees as cover. In the centre was a small clearing where a ruined house stood. The ramshackle cottage was now crawling with dogs. They were all different sizes and colours. To one side lay a large pile of bones, some looked human.

Chris slipped back and nodded to Marty. They leant close together like lovers ready to kiss.

"Loads of the buggers," Chris breathed.

"Loads as in a lot, or loads as in massive?" Marty hissed back.

"Too many really. I got an idea though." Chris tugged on Marty's sleeve and led him around the car. Squatting down he drew a rough map in the dirt.

"So, there's a house there?" Marty asked.

"Yep. That's the killer. We can't just bomb them. That house will protect them."

"We gotta shoot them then?"

"We can do better then that. You go east. The wind's from that way. Take a couple of smoke bombs. Set them off, then double back to the car. I'm gonna set up some proxy bombs, so when they run this way that should thin their numbers."

"Then what?"

Chris smiled. "We finish what's left. Time to give Fido a thrashing. Get three smokes and lob them near the house, but don't get too close. And watch out for any strays wandering around."

Marty nodded and took three green grenades from one of the metal boxes. Chris waited until he was out of sight behind the trees, then lifted four metal blocks from another bin. These had lettering to say which way to plant them. Using the 'Front towards enemy' side facing inwards Chris set them to cause maximum damage should the pack run into the thin tripwires.

Doubling back he heard the soft pop of the smokes. The dogs began their barking, some sounded angry, others scared. Chris took some grenades and lined them up on the flat wing of the car. He pulled the pins out, then put them back so only the tip was still in. he also laid ten rifle magazines on the bonnet, ready to use. Finally he leant the two spare rifles against the car, each loaded with a full magazine. If they had a stoppage they could drop their rifle and get a new one.

Chapter 7

Marty jogged around the car. "Smoke's gone."

"I can see." Chris waved at the woods. Thin wisps of grey smoke floated in the still day from the trees. The barking intensified.

"Looks like I threw them the right way," Marty said, pleased with himself.

"More like they have one way in and out."

"Maybe. Pretty stupid to do that."

"They ain't too smart." Chris watched the tree line down the iron sights of his rifle. The barking was growing, then silenced by a loud bang. It resumed, but another bang cut the intensity again.

"Claymores?" Marty asked.

"Bloody good, ain't they?"

"Hell yeah."

A lone dog ran out, heading for the rolling grasslands. Chris let it run, then dropped it with a single shot. More broke from the trees, hurried by another explosion. Both men stood and opened fire. Magazines were emptied, then dropped as full ones were loaded. Barrels glowed a dull red as they spat round after round into the pack. Marty couldn't believe that many dogs existed. Chris shouted something and threw his rifle down. Marty yelled back and kept firing while Chris took one of the spares.

Their hands ached from pulling the triggers and their shoulders were throbbing, but still the dog pack continued. A fourth thud told them the last proxy bomb had gone off. Marty paused to throw the grenades into the bulk of the pack. When the magazines ran out Marty had to jump on the small machine gun, leaving Chris to throw the last of the grenades. Exhausted they saw the last of the dogs run out, and fall. Chris waved Marty to stay where he was, before taking the last spare rifle and moving forwards.

He kept to a half stoop, rifle raised. He walked past the bodies of the pack, ignoring the few that still moved. Instead he headed into the still smoking woods. Marty heard occasional shots, but he checked the machine gun over, grimacing at the nearly empty ammo box.

Chris came out the woods with his rifle still raised. This time he checked the dead, shooting the wounded. With a tired smile he nodded to Marty, then leant on the car.

"Bloody hell, that was intense."

Marty leant back in his seat. "You're telling me. Another minute and we'd have been out of ammo."

"Really?"

"Nearly empty," Marty said, tapping the metal ammo box.

"Bugger. We really gotta do a replen run."

Chris laid out the rifles on the bonnet, checking one worked before tasking Marty with cleaning the others.

"How bad are we?" Marty asked.

"Bad. Got fuel and food ok, but that just wiped us out of ammo for everything save a few mags and the big gun."

"What about grenades?"

"That was it." Chris sighed. "Hell of a session. Get them rifles cleaned and reload some mags, then we can get our tails."

It took an hour to strip and clean the weapons, Chris keeping a watch all around. That much noise would attract attention. Once they were ready Chris handed his rifle to Marty, and took his knife from his belt. he began unenthusiastically cutting the tails from the pack. Three hours later they slung the last of the tails into the back.

"Need a bigger car," Marty said.

"Or smaller prey," Chris added.

"That would help. Shame we don't get paid by the tail."

"We get paid enough. Whatever meat they have cured can go in our chiller once we get back."

"How long until we get home?"

Chris started the car and drove away, leaving the bodies for the flies. "Be a full day tomorrow. Best be getting a good night's sleep tonight. We need to be up early tomorrow."

"I'll sleep well."

"I mean it. No fillies tonight."

Marty groaned. "Not even one?"

"Only one."

"How about three?"

Chris punched Marty on the shoulder, smiling when the younger man swore. He had hit the bruise from the rifle recoil.

"One. Final offer."

"Ok, one."

"And you're doing the dinner." Chris relaxed. Their quarry was disposed of, their reward was waiting for them, and they were alive. True, they had to do an urgent replenishment run to the bunker, but they had done the job. That was all that mattered. He drove them back to the village in silence, Marty pouting about the curfew imposed by the early start.

Chapter 8

They reached the village just before dark, Chris driving carefully to save them losing the tails. The elder was shocked at how many they had brought with them, even asking if they were all from the same pack. Once he was convinced they were he doubled the reward payment. The young boy and his family took one of the tails and hung it from the door of their hut, a sign that they had lost a member, but avenged the loss.

Some of the villagers laid the tails out and began chanting. They knelt in a circle around the pile and looked to the sky, arms held high.

"What they doing?" Marty asked.

"Giving thanks," Chris said.

Some of the group made marks in the dirt, either of a fish or and X. others just chanted in some strange language.

"They talking a curse or something?" Marty asked, taking a step back.

"No. they're speaking from their souls."

"Souls? What's a soul?"

Chris smiled. "You never went into a prayer house?"

"Never. Don't need some spooky god watching me while I work. I stay away from them, they stay away from me."

"You never learn, really."

"What's that supposed to mean?"

Chris shook his head and knelt with the group. They seemed surprised at first, then shuffled aside to let him in. to Marty's amazement Chris held his hands up and spoke in a loud voice words Marty couldn't understand. The elder watched with an impressed expression as Chris raised his voice with the others. They cried and swayed until all of them collapsed. Marty went to help Chris, but another villager held him back. Uncertain, Marty waited, impatiently tapping one hand on his hip, near his pistol. After an eternity Chris stood up.

"Wow," he said, brushing the dust off his camouflaged trousers. "Not done that in a while."

"Done what?" Marty asked, almost an accusation.

"Spoke in my spirit, to the Spirit."

"What Spirit?"

"The only spirit you know is one you drink. This is more, well, deeper."

Marty looked half ready to cry, half ready to explode. "Deeper?"

"I'll tell you later. Nice to see some places still believe. Let's camp down for the night. Early start tomorrow." Chris left Marty watching the circle of people while he parked the car beside the wall, stringing his hammock from a roof beam of a mud hut.

"So, what were you saying?" Marty asked when Chris was finished.

"When?"

"Just then, on the ground."

"Oh. No idea really. It just comes out."

"Sounds like you knew."

Chris shrugged, smiling. "Not really. It's not my mind speaking, it's my soul."

"Sounds like that weird madman we saw last cycle. You know, the one who kept heads on his belt and shouted curses?"

"He was an interesting bloke."

"Very. He said I would be cursed for sleeping with all those girls," Marty said with near pride. "That didn't happen."

"Because he wasn't speaking from his soul, just his head."

"So what does your soul say?"

"I haven't a clue. I just know it asks for things for me, and they happen."

Marty looked lost. "You don't know what it asks, but it asks for stuff and you get it? How the hell does that work?"

"Don't strain the brain. It just does."

"I thought you only had faith in yourself?"

Chris lifted his rifle from the holder behind the front seats. "I have faith in this, in myself and where my soul leads me. Half of what we do is thinking about what we are doing. The other half is instinct."

"Ah," Marty said, enlightenment making his face glow. "So your soul guides you in life?"

"Pretty much. Tells me when to stay put, or move on."

"What's it saying now?"

Chris checked the rifle over. "It says 'shut up Marty and get some work done'."

"Thanks soul," Marty said. He took his rifle and went to walk the wall while Chris cleaned his own rifle. It had already been stripped and cleaned after they had killed the dog pack, but Chris liked to be sure.

Marty came back with a girl. He waited until Chris nodded his permission, then Marty left with the girl, taking only his pistol. Chris watched him go, the village elder waving a thankful hand as he passed Marty.

"I wish to thank you again," the elder said to Chris.

"It's no bother."

"I know, but to us it means more than that. You have given us peace. Your reputation stands firm."

"Thanks, but I'm not too bothered about my reputation."

The elder poked the half stripped rifle that Chris had laid out on the bonnet. "Your reputation should be a concern to you. Good reputations are a tool, like your weapons. A bad reputation is a curse. It can hold you back."

"All that holds me back is the hours of the day, and the capacity of my magazines."

"You are a Hunter. That carries weight. But you could be more. I take it you are going to enter the trials?"

Chris shook his head and began reassembling the rifle. "I don't care for public events. I just want to do my job and get paid."

"They are coming up soon, and with your weapons you should be an easy winner." The elder watched with his head canted to one side, a sly smile on his face. "Think of the riches you could win."

"What good is trinkets to a man like me?"

"What about the fame, the pride you will have should you win?"

"Fame buys nothing and pride is for fools." Chris felt tense, the conversation becoming tiring.

The elder pressed him still. "Your reputation would be set in stone. You would be the best Hunter in the land. Prove to yourself you can be the best."

"And what would that achieve?"

"For the world, very little. But for you? Maybe nothing, maybe everything. There's only one way to find out."

"Why are you going on about this?" Chris asked, putting the assembled rifle down hard.

"If I were a friend to the best Hunter in the lands, I would have better prospects for service from all the others, and better protection for my village."

Chris laughed. "I see your point. Sorry, but I'm not into fame and popularity. If I entered that contest, it wouldn't be for that."

"What would it be for then?"

"For myself, and myself isn't fussed about titles."

"Your choice," the elder said, stepping back. "I only wanted to know, in case some of the small amount of gold we have could be wagered on your victory."

"Save your money," Chris said. "It would be better served on a travelling merchant. Buy a new plough and your village will be better served."

"I will. Thank you, Hunter ." The elder held out a hand, then left. Chris watched him go, amused. The idea of being the greatest Hunter would be amusing, but he didn't do it for fame or fortune. He worked because he enjoyed it, and he made the difference. That was his reward, and that was all he needed.

Chapter 9

The cold morning mist hung to the ground, defying the sun.
Jake was already up, washing pots from the night before. The fire
was embracing and warm, and Jake didn't mind tidying up. The
water was hot in the large iron cauldron, so Jake scooped some
of it up with an earthen bowl and rinsed the dirty bowls with the
water. Tipping the used water onto the hard packed dirt Jake
swilled and rinsed until they were all clean, then used a stick to
clean the cauldron. He tipped the still hot water out using his
own shirt to protect his hands.

To the outsider Jake looked every bit an alien, someone who
didn't come from here. Where most villagers made do with
animal skins and scavenged rags, Jake wore the rough weave
clothes he had worn when he worked the farms. His trousers
were a brown denim, with large pockets, and loops on the waist
for carrying tools. Even the threadbare cloth looked more official
than the rough furs worn by villagers. Some of the bigger villages

had access to cloth, but usually it was saved for special occasions.

Ben staggered out of a hut and groaned, twisting his back straight. He shivered against the morning cold, and took a stinking fur pelisse from the hut.

"What you doing?" Ben asked, getting as close to the fire as he could.

"Just a few odd jobs."

"Odd jobs? You wanna live here?"

Jake shook his head, sending his long blondish hair flailing. "Just wanna make sure they miss us."

"Yeah, right. Any food out here?"

"How can you be hungry after last night?"

"What can I say?" Ben said with a sly smile. "It's a gift. Food?"

"No idea. I've not been up long myself. Where's our leader?"

"Greg? You know after a night like last night he ain't gonna be up early."

Jake knew that was true. They had killed the Allosaurus 4 days ago, but Greg seldom went anywhere unless he had to. They could be here for weeks, eating the village stores empty. Usually it was when Greg grew tired of the women that they left.

"So we staying another night?" Jake asked.

"Not for too much longer. The Boss wants to go to the city, for the Trials."

"We really going for them?"

"You think of a good reason why not?"

Jake tried, and gave in. "Not really. Just, well."

Ben caught the unsaid words. "Just what?"

"Well, you know?" Jake sighed. "I'm worried."

"About what?"

"It's Greg."

Ben laughed. "You're worried about Greg? I'm not. Why should we? He can take care of himself."

"That's just the point. He can, but he's so, kinda, well he's a bit over the top."

"That's his style. Give them a show, a bit of flair. That's his middle name after all."

"I know," Jake said, nodding. He stared at the fire. "Greg 'Flair' Numlok, Master Hunter."

"And when he wins, he will be *the* Master Hunter."

"What about the others?"

Ben scoffed, dropping another stick on the fire. "Kids with clubs? Seriously? They're never gonna outshine Greg."

"There's the one with the flash sticks."

"He's dead. I heard it said. Went after something massive and it got 'im instead." Ben clenched his teeth. "Just shut it about the Boss. Ok, so he's a bit of an arse, and he has his head up there too. But he can do the job, and do it better than anyone else. In a week or two he will be titled as such, so just follow along."

"Is that how you survive?" Jake poked the fire, shuffling back from the flames.

"Yeah. That's how I survive. Truth be told he gets on my tits occasionally. I know he does it for show, but I sometimes think do we need that much show?"

"Yeah. Still, it works for him I guess." Jake grew bolder as he realised Ben felt the same way.

"We just gotta keep 'im out of trouble. Be his eyes and ears as it were."

"I think we can do that."

"Sounds a plan." Ben stood and kicked dirt on the fire. "Because it works both ways. Stop pissing around out here and get some sleep."

"Ok," Jake said. He stood and went back to his hut. The sounds of heavy snoring showed Greg was still asleep.

As a Hunter, Greg was a skilled showman. He even looked the part, with his massive muscles, shining blades, and commanding voice. The ladies love the body, topped with auburn hair and soft brown eyes. Greg even dressed the part, walking around like a mythical Hunter in furs and cowhide belts. Jake was envious of Greg, that he would never deny. But he didn't want to be Greg. He wanted to be a Hunter, but a one who came, did the job, and left. The village was too scared to ask them to leave. No elder would risk his village by upsetting a Hunter. But they had stayed far too long, and the big feasts that were laid out each night would leave the villagers short later on this year. That troubled Jake, and he slowly drifted into an uncomfortable sleep.

"Wakey wakey sunshine, time to get to work."

The familiar voice tugged at Marty's conscious, pulling him out from his dreams. He didn't want to leave.

"Oh, crap! Marty! Run!"

The urgent shout woke him in an instant. Marty rolled out of his hammock and drew his pistol. Kneeling on the dirt beside the Land Rover he looked all around, seeking the danger. All he saw was a sleeping village, and a near hysterical Chris.

"That's rather childlike," Marty said, brushing the dirt from his knee and holstering his pistol.

"You wouldn't wake up," Chris said, tears rolling down his cheeks.

"Could have tried something more subtle."

"I don't do subtle," Chris said with pride.

"True. I've heard your snoring."

"You're obsessed with that. Seriously, you gotta let it go."

"Only if I get some of those ear covers to block the sound."

"Then I will need to kick you out of bed in the morning." Chris nodded to the small fire he had built. A metal tin of hot water steamed beside the flames. Marty had a quick shave while Chris did his checks on the car. Once the fire was out, the hammocks packed away, and everything locked down they drove out the gates and headed north-west. The morning mists hid a lot of the detail, but Chris knew the way. He had been driving these plains for the past few years, and even when he was lost the sun and the moon were his guides. He just kept going until he found something familiar.

They followed the main convoy route, the road was smoother and better running. They saw a convoy coming the other way from a nearby trade post, but they didn't care much for the news so they didn't press for a news scroll. As the sun rose so did the temperature. Layers that had been put on to stave off the cold were slowly shed until they were down to short sleeves. Chris kept an eye on the fuel gauge, just in case.

Marty kept his eye on the horizon. Usually it was only raiders who attacked at first light, but you couldn't be sure. They were too low on ammo to have a sustained attack, so running was their best option. The sooner they knew they had to run, the easier it would be.

"So, how long we gonna be back home?" Marty asked.

"I'm thinking a week or so. Wanna check the bunker for some parts for this, and do a full clean out."

"We not doing the Trials then?"

Chris shot him a glance. "I ain't gonna parade around like a prize bull for them to applaud and score me. What you think we'll get out of it? Some fat mayor come up and give us a small trophy. What use is that?"

"Just thought we would win, you know."

"We may, that's true. But why should we? We don't need to advertise so we don't need to win any Trial. And what if we lose? Think of the embarrassment."

"How can we lose?"

"Politics. You know how those cities run. Hell, we spent too long in two of them and only just made it out of the last one."

"That was different," Marty said.

"How?"

Marty opened his mouth, then closed it again. "I don't know. I just wanna do it. See what the other Hunters are like."

"And get some prize fillies too no doubt."

"There is that."

"Is women all you care about?" Chris asked.

Marty shook his head slowly. "Not the only thing. I care about food too."

"Not me then. Thanks."

"Hey, if you were more attractive I might care about you too."

"You like walking, don't you?" Chris asked with a sly smile.

"Yeah. Why?"

"Because you're gonna do a hell of a lot of it if you keep talking."

"Meh," Marty replied, sticking his tongue out.

"We ain't doing the Trials," Chris said after a few minutes silence.

"I know. Just woulda been nice to have tried."

"Some dozy mayor telling us how good we are? I value the opinion of the elder who's village we save."

"True." Marty suddenly brightened. "Say, if the other Hunters are at this Trial thing, then we get free roam of the villages."

"We do anyway."

"Yeah, but this time we don't have to worry about meeting any of them."

Chris laughed. "We don't worry anyway. Sticks and stones against us? C'mon. not exactly much competition."

"So, we would win the Trials easily."

Chris went serious. "Right, drop it. We ain't doing the Trials. Shut it before I really do make you walk."

Marty lapsed back into silence and they let the miles rumble under them as they headed away from the rising sun.

Chapter 10

The clatter of metal on stone woke Jake from a dream he was happy to leave. Hobbling into the heat of the sun he saw Greg was using the town's whetstone to sharpen his blades. Jake knew it would take a while to do all the blades, so he left Greg with his crowd of onlookers and went to find Ben.

"I hate this thing sometimes," Ben said, kicking their cart.

"What's up with it now?" Jake asked, keeping his distance.

"That mount thing has gone again."

"The thing that we pull it with?"

Ben made a face that only showed his irritation in greater clarity. "Not the shafts. I'm talking about the pivot thing that they attach to. The metal mount has cracked again. We can't go too far until it's fixed."

"Can it be fixed?"

"Not much choice, really."

Greg loped over, his flamboyant gait half for show, half due to an old injury.

"What's going on?" Greg asked. His auburn hair wafted as he walked, and the voice made Jake feel things he shouldn't.

"Blasted mount is going again." Ben kicked a wheel again.

"Well, fix it then."

"How?" Ben held both hands out wide, bending forwards as if greeting royalty. "If you have a way to solve this then please, feel free to offer your advice."

"There must be a metal man here someplace," Greg said, half to himself. "All we need is to find him, and get him to fix the cart."

"Great. Go do it then." Ben threw his hands in the air and stormed off. "As if I hadn't thought of that," drifted back to them on the still air.

"Child," Greg said, waving dismissively at Ben's back. "Big child. So, Jake. What you think about this? We gonna get ourselves a fixer man to fix it?"

"I have every faith in you, Greg." Jake blushed and felt ashamed.

"Of course you do. Go find him for me." Greg turned in the dirt, one cowhide soled sandal grating dust. He loped back to the hut, the screams from inside showed he wasn't bored of this village yet.

"Go find him," Jake muttered to himself. He looked at the cart, then to Greg's hut, then to Ben's. Shrugging his shoulders he went to see the elder.

There wasn't anyone who could fix the cart in the village. A travelling merchant usually patched the cauldron, and any other tools they used, but he hadn't been seen in months. Jake asked in vain until he gave in. nobody could fix the cart. When he came back to the cart he saw Ben was already working on it.

"Finally," Ben said, crouched under the cart looking at the front axle. "Where the bloody hell you been?"

"Finding a fixer man," Jake said.

"Why?"

"To fix the cart." Jake felt stupid saying it, and Ben looked at him in a way that said he didn't disagree with Jake's feelings..

"I'm fixing the cart," Ben said. "Me. All by my lonesome too. You gonna do any work around here?"

"I was," Jake protested.

"Yeah. Get me a mallet from the kit box."

Jake held back childish tears and instead rummaged for the soft wooden mallet. He handed it to Ben, who didn't thank him. A few hard bangs and a metal pin dropped to the floor.

"Now then," Ben said, coming out from under the cart. "Here's where you make up for going walkies. I'm gonna lift the front of the cart. You roll the axle out."

Jake nodded and laid his hands on one of the wooden wheel spokes. When Ben frowned, but kept silent Jake braced himself. With effort, muscles straining, Ben lifted the front of the cart. Jake rolled the axle forwards, but Ben was in the way.

"What you doing?" Ben hissed through clenched teeth.

"Rolling the axle out," Jake said.

"Not with me here."

"Well, what you suggest?"

Ben moaned and lowered the cart onto the axle, letting the shafts support the weight of the cart. Ben massaged his arms.

"You roll it backwards, you donkey."

"Sorry," Jake said. "Why would I roll it backwards? The other axle is in the way."

Ben sneered. "You roll it backwards so I can lower the front."

"Then it will be on the axle still."

Ben went to speak, then realised Jake was right. "Ok, genius. We both lift the cart, and roll the axle out. You think that will work?"

"Yeah," Jake replied, countering the sarcastic tone with a smile.

"Yeah, he says. Get your side."

They lifted the cart and rolled the axle out, Jake struggling to hold the cart with one hand. He was relieved when Ben said to lower it down. Taking more tools Ben removed the cracked mount and told Jake to stoke a fire. Using the heat Ben managed to hammer the crack together, using bits of metal to brace it. When it had cooled they lifted the cart again, Jake trembling under the weight. Ben then lifted it by himself while Jake went underneath and lined up the mount. The generous covering of animal fat made the mount slide in easily, and soon the cart was back together.

"All fixed?" Greg said, emerging from his hut."

Ben wiped his dirty face in the setting sun. "All fixed, Boss. We got a job?"

"Always have a job," Greg beamed. "We leave in the morning."

"Where for?" Jake asked.

"Glad you asked, shows keenness. We are doing the Trials, naturally. They can't have a challenge without me there." Greg struck one of his victory poses, mostly for the watching villagers.

"It will take that long to get there?" Ben asked, throwing tools back into the box.

"It will. A long walk and we need to stock up on provisions. I don't think there are many villages between us and the Trials." Greg spoke loudly, making sure the elder could hear.

"Take all you need, Hunter," the elder said, coming closer.

"Very gracious of you," Greg replied, half bowing. "All we need is water mostly, and some cured meat naturally."

"It will be given to you first thing in the morning, Hunter."

Greg thanked the elder, gently ushered him away, then waved Ben and Jake closer.

"We need to get stocked up as the country gets a bit hilly later, and if we're gonna make this Trial we need to have our strength. Ben, you can pull while Jake pushes." Greg stood back, waiting their responses.

"Sure," Ben said after a pause. "What about getting ourselves a mule?"

Greg scoffed and waved a dismissive hand. "Just another mouth to feed. We have more than enough here to get us to the Trials."

"And you will be riding on the cart?" Jake asked.

"Naturally," Greg answered, that confident smile seemed a permanent fixture. "I need to conserve my strength for the Trials. Can't be turning up worn out from the walk."

Greg clapped them both on the back, and went back to his hut.

"Amazed he has strength left after all those women," Jake said when the screams started again.

"True, but he's gotta do the Trials, not us," Ben agreed. "So we take care of him."

"He better bleeding walk on the hilly bits."

"Doubt that," Ben said. Jake nodded, and they checked the wooden boxes on the cart, making sure all their equipment and clothes were secure. It would be an early night so they had all day tomorrow to get as many miles done as possible.

Chapter 11

The bunker was just as they had left it. Marty often wondered how Chris first found it. The underground structure was hidden by a dense forest, the opening cut into the hillside. Chris had made sure the shutter door was well maintained, and used the paint in the massive storerooms to keep it camouflaged.

They drove around the bunker in a big circle to hide their tracks, then drove to the door. Marty sat behind the big gun while Chris went with his rifle to check his traps. Satisfied nobody had been here Chris opened the small door to get inside. After a long minute the shutter door rolled open with a soft metallic squeal, like a dark mouth opening.

Inside it was inky black, but when Chris drove the car in the lights came on, blasting the darkness away and illuminating everything in perfect detail. Parking the car, Chris closed the door and set to work. Together they found all the ammunition they needed, and piled it near the car. Then they checked the spare parts and replaced all they felt they needed to. Then Marty refuelled the car and their metal fuel cans from the hidden tanks. Chris went to find a spare engine.

"Any joy?" Marty asked when Chris came back.

"Not a sign of one," Chris said. He was streaked with dust and sweat, having spent the past hour scrambling around crates.

"Sucks. So what you gonna do?"

"Either rebuild it again, or take one out of another car."

Marty slid the full fuel can into it's holder on the car and looked around him. There were plenty of cars to choose from. Lined up were rows of Land Rovers like theirs, most with cabs or at least a roof on. There were trailers, metal storage boxes, massive cars with tracks instead of wheels, and at the back was the biggest mystery. There sat the metal birds, silent with giant wings. Chris wanted to learn how they flew, but didn't want to die doing it, so they lay there in the air conditioned bunker, waiting.

"We good?" Chris asked, waving at the fuel can.

"Yeah. Just about to do a full clear out."

"Let's do it then."

Together they removed the weapons, laying them near the ammo. Then they took each storage box and emptied them out. Repacking everything Chris inspected each item, tossing it away if it looked suspicious. It took most of the night, but they managed it. When the car was ready to go they went to the empty barrack rooms and collapsed into a satisfied but exhausted sleep.

The next morning Marty woke first. He left Chris snoring in his bunk and went to the gym. In the large padded room Marty stripped to the waist and looked over the dull metal weights. Chris preferred the rolling floor to the weights, the ability to run without going anywhere helped his fitness, but not his appearance. Marty to himself inside that how they look should reflect how they work. A powerful body means a powerful Hunter. Chris would have laughed had Marty mentioned this, explaining that their guns were their tools, not their bodies. Chris was happy so long as he could outrun whatever was chasing him.

Marty started on the rolling floor machine, the rubber belt squeaked a little, but ran smooth enough. After working up a sweat Marty slowed down, then did a burst of speed. This made the heart pound, but also made him feel stronger. Once he was done on the rolling floor machine, leaning on the rails that ran down the sides to catch his breath, Marty went to the weights.

The designers of the gym had put mirrors down one wall from floor to ceiling. Marty didn't know why, maybe to stop people bumping into each other while they exercised. Instead, he used them to see how he looked when he worked out. Lifting, pushing, rolling and straining, Marty worked himself until his arms trembled, and he felt like he couldn't lift his hands. There was fatigue in his arms, but there was also power, the same as you feel after running, tired, but knowing you can do it again once rested. Marty stood before the mirror wall and stretched.

"You look like you've crapped yourself," Chris said.

"I look better than you do," Marty shot back, picking up one of the green towels and wiping his face.

"Yeah, whatever." Chris went onto the rolling floor machine, smiling at the settings Marty had used. Chris was more of a distance runner. He could move fast over short distance, his job depended on that. When you had something chasing you the best thing to do was build up as big a lead as possible.

Some things gave in quickly, like most of the dinos and the raiders that roamed in bands. The dog packs were the worst.

Once, one pack had chased the Land Rover for nearly an hour. Determined not to be the dog's dinner, Chris had upped his exercise routine, even jogging around villages when they were out working.

Chris set the machine to his level and began jogging. There was a screen mounted on the machine, presumably for the jogger to watch, but it didn't work. Some electrics Chris could understand, but not monitors. When he had found the bunker he was lost, tired, and ready to die. His village had been destroyed, his family killed, his home was turned to rubble. He had run from the village, and kept running. Once in the trees he felt safer, but he didn't have any food or water. For what seemed like days he roamed, until he fell across the bunker. It took nearly a year, but he taught himself to read, and to use the equipment. He was still learning, but now Chris could understand the technical manuals in the bunker, and he could repair the cars and weapons. That was enough for him, for now.

"You just jogging?" Marty asked, still shaking the ache from his arms.

"Yeah. No point doing anything else."

"You sure? Be good if you had some meat on you."

"I got meat," Chris said.

"On your body," Marty pointed out.

"There too."

Marty shook his head, grinning. "You really don't wanna look like this?" he asked, flexing his arms.

"What good is that if you can't hold a rifle because your muscles are too big?"

"They ain't too big," Marty said, looking at himself in the mirror.

"They will be if you keep it up."

"Just because you can't do the weight I lift."

Chris stopped the machine and walked over to the weights. "This the best you can lift?" he asked, looking at a thick metal bar. The weight discs on the ends were thicker than his wrist, and there were a lot of them.

"That's my best," Marty said with pride.

Chris shrugged, stooped, and lifted the weights. He first rolled them up his chest, then braced his legs so he could lift the bar over his head. Rolling it back down he stooped again and dropped the bar onto the padded floor with a soft clang.

"Not bad, I guess," Chris said, walking out. Marty stared open mouthed from the weights to Chris' back. What he didn't see was that when Chris walked out the door he paused and held his back, moaning. Limping slightly Chris hobbled back to bed. Marty just looked at the weights, testing them with his foot.

Chapter 12

Greg lay on the cart and waved. Jake and Ben pushed the shafts while their leader promised to come back one day, and he would always treasure them. Some of the girls who had kept him company waved a tearful farewell. Once on the road the cart rolled over the rough dirt road. They avoided the main convoy roads, knowing the fast moving lorries could smash their wooden cart without even noticing it. Instead they used the tracks made by the travelling merchants. There were a lot of them about, usually in covered carts pulled by a mule or a skinny cow.

"How long we got to go?" Jake asked Ben, his face already damp with sweat.

"Long enough," Ben replied. "We got plenty of hills to do so we may as well practice with this one."

"You guys ok down there?" Greg asked, chewing on some cured meat.

"Yeah, Boss," Ben said. "Just thinking about rest stops. We got a long ways to go."

"True. You guys need to stop then do so. Just keep the cart rolling steady. I need my sleep." Greg spat the half chewed meat out and rolled himself in a rough blanket.

"Steady?" Jake asked quietly.

"As in smooth, not bumpy," Ben replied.

"Hope these Trials are worth it."

"They will be. Think of the food and drink when we get there."

Jake looked skywards. "Roast meats, fresh bread, and milk."

"And maybe even a cake."

"Cakes?" Jake near yelped. "I haven't had a cake since we left home. A real cake, with a cream filling."

"And jam," Ben reminded.

"And jam. It's been too long since my last cake."

Ben clicked his tongue. "And beer."

"Oh, beer!" Jake walked with his mouth open, tongue lolling. "Cold, frothy, inebriating beer."

"In a proper wooden tankard, with foam rolling down the sides."

"I could murder a beer right now."

"Remember that village with the home brew?" Ben asked.

"Not too much of it," Jake said, making them both laugh.

"Me neither, but I do remember how good it was."

"We should have stayed there."

"Hell, I can't remember where the hell it was."

"Me neither."

"Maybe one day," Ben said.

"One day."

They walked in silence, the hill still lying ahead of them more than it did behind. The sun was getting hotter, and the dry plains were still and hot.

"Just on last Beer," Jake said and the cart rumbled along, one man dreaming of women and glory, two others daydreamed about cold beer and warm bread.

Chris was up first, and decided to check the levels in the fuel and water tanks. They could, and did survive from water they found in streams and wells, but fuel was a different matter. Chris once tried using lamp oil and it made the car run badly and smoke like a damp wood fire.

The tanks were submerged deep under the concrete floor of the bunker. Only the pumps and dispensers were visible. Chris checked the levels on the old, round gauges and clicked his tongue. Fuel was fine, even the volatile tanks of something called 'aviation fuel' were holding up well. It was the water tanks. They seemed to be contaminated with something. Chris didn't know what was wrong, but the water tasted foul, like something had died in there.

Opening up the pump cabinet Chris took a head torch and went down into the tank. The smell grew worse and soon he found the problem. There was a tree root growing through the metal and polymer skin of the tank. This had let dirt and whatever else had sunk into the soil drain through into the water. With a sigh Chris climbed back out. He had manuals to read. Marty was waiting at the top of the ladder.

"Arrgh!" Chris shrieked, startled by Marty's head as it popped into view.

"I ain't that ugly," Marty protested.

"You are. Hideous. Worse than any dino."

"You're a dino. I'm awesome."

"So says you." Chris dropped the head torch onto the top of the water pump and shook his head.

""I'm awesome. Ask any of the women we meet."

"I would, but they all suddenly go silent after a night with you."

"Because they are in awe of my manliness," Marty beamed.

"More depressed they were that desperate."

"At least I get some trim. You get your hammock."

"Reliable," Chris said, heading for the library.

"What you up to, anyway?" Marty asked, following Chris.

"Water tank has a leak. Need to see how to weld it."

"Just use a welder, like normal." Marty leant on a table in the small library, looking over the spines of textbooks.

"Not simple. There's a coating on it to stop the water rotting the metal. Need to find out what it is and how to fix it."

"Good luck."

"Hey. You get to studying. Don't think I ain't seen you in that gym and not here."

"I fight with my body, not my brains," Marty said, lingering by the door.

"Your brain controls your body, so make it stronger." Chris found the manual he needed, and pointed at a chair for Marty to sit.

Marty threw his hands into the air and let out a dramatic sigh, but he sat anyway. Chris slid a book from the fiction area over the metal tabletop, then flicked through his manual. Once he'd found the details of the tanks he looked up the repair method.

It often surprised Chris at how well this place had lasted. The air was still clean, the lights mostly worked, and the equipment was almost perfect. He knew there was something called air conditioning that took water out of the air and made things drier. That stopped the rot. True, some of the rubber items like tyres and boot soles were perished, but on the whole everything had been stored to last, and last it had.

Even the fuel, in three massive tanks, had been treated to stop it going off, although it was slowly degrading, making the car smoke and splutter. Chris had found ways to counter this, and each fuel can was laced with paraffin oil or petroleum to water down the thick diesel. The motor oil was in sealed cans, only needing a good shake to mix it properly. It was mostly the paints and tins of oil based items that separated, needing a lot of vigorous shaking and stirring to mix them properly. The food was vacuum sealed and lasted well even in heat.

Finally, the ammunition was in it's own locker, a massive walk-in cupboard that held racks and racks of metal boxes, each with up to 500 rounds per box. There were grenades, rockets, launchers and proximity bombs. Everything an army would need, all sealed and protected. All forgotten, until Chris found it.

He went to the big maintenance bay and found the chemicals he needed. Knowing the water in the tank was bad, Chris first pumped the tank dry, letting it run off while he mixed the sealant for the tank. Then he cut out the damaged section, and cut back the tree root. Lacing the ground with old sump oil and poison he hoped to kill the tree off. How the root had found it's way this deep was a mystery, but he didn't want it coming back.

Once the root was dealt with Chris took a sheet of steel from the maintenance bay, fingers slipping on the oiled surface. He tack welded it into place, leaving a small hole in the top. Once the plate was fully welded into place Chris poured a mix of concrete and sealant mix through the hole, hoping it would not only fill the hole, but also highlight any small holes in his welding. It didn't leak, so Chris painted the inside with the sealant, glad it was low on the tank and he didn't have to stand too high up.

"Looks good," Marty called from the manhole above, his voice echoing.

"Yeah. You done your reading for today?"

"All of it."

"Why you sweating then?"

"Wanted to work my body after my brain, you know, to balance them out."

Chris rolled his eyes. "You get down here, muscle boy, and give me hand to clean up. Need to change the filters on the pump, then we can fill this tank up tomorrow."

Marty came down the ladder, helping to lift the bent piece of metal Chris had removed.

"You know," Marty said. "I've been thinking."

"That's a worry."

"C'mon. Be serious."

Chris leant on the wall of the tank, feeling his face grow damp with sweat. "What about?"

"Them trials." Marty held out a hand when Chris opened his mouth. "Look, I know you don't wanna do it," he started.

"Damn right."

"But we should, if only to see what would happen."

"You know about curiosity?"

"Is that a meal?"

Chris punched Marty on the arm gently. "It killed the cat."

"What cat? Anyway, I wanna see what these Trials are about."

"Good luck, then," Chris said, picking up a broom and sweeping the floor of the tank.

"That's it? After all we've been through that's all you're gonna say?"

"What you want me to say?"

"That you'll come with me."

Chris leant on the broom. "Just say we go, and we win. Then what? Won't make a difference out here."

"But we will know. What's the worst that can happen?"

"Where do I start?"

Marty held both hands out. "Ok, then how about this? We go, look, and leave. We don't need to do them, just have a peep."

"Last time you said that we ended up naked in a prison cell, remember?"

"True, but it was a laugh."

Chris stared into Marty's eyes, reading them. "Ok, we go, if only for some peace. Now shut up and go get the car ready. If we're gonna go, we gotta head first thing in the morning."

"Yes, Boss," Marty said, leaping up the ladder.

"I must be mad," Chris said to the broom, which didn't reply.

Chapter 13

The next day Ben and Jake saw the high walls of the city. Like most cities this one didn't have a name, most either knowing it for what it produced, or who controlled it. Being situated on the coast this city was known for fishing and preserving the fish. The smell of salt was strong even before they saw the high patched walls.

All the big cities had walls, some larger than others. Like the villages these walls protected the inhabitants. The larger cities used stone and rubble from nearby settlements when the world order fell, building massive defensive walls to keep marauding factions away. All the weapons were used up, until there were only blades and clubs left. This made the walls almost redundant, any attacking group couldn't breach them. Instead the world calmed as everyone settled into a new life, and the cities became centres for trade and manufacturing. They were strict, not allowing outsiders to move in. They were also crime free. Anyone convicted of even the smallest of crimes was expelled, condemned to die in the outside world that they knew nothing about. Only the convoy lorries came and went, and they were kept to the edge.

The walls seemed massive, but Ben and Jake knew they would be truly breathtaking up close. Most villages had walls twice the height of a man, to keep wild animals and the few bands of wild raiders out. These stone and rubble walls were easily ten times higher, with massive gates made of wood or metal to protect them. Inside, it was a different world, one of comfort and luxury. No Hunter went to a big city. They didn't need the Hunter, and the Hunter certainly had no need of their services.

They pulled the cart along, Greg snoring loudly on the back. A bump in the road woke him.

"Wassat?" Greg said, rolling over on his blanket bed.

"The Trials," Ben said. Greg rolled off the cart and landed nimbly on his feet. He walked alongside.

"Trials, eh? Looks like a decent place where I can shine. What are those buildings by the wall?"

"Looks like some sort of tent village," Jake said, his young eyes were able to see better.

"Well," Greg said, "I won't be sleeping there. I'm sure they will have some nice stone hut for me inside the walls."

"I'm sure," Ben said, half convinced.

Greg smiled and rolled back onto the cart. In moments he was snoring again.

"Where do we sleep?" Jake asked.

"Where we are supposed to sleep, at the foot of his bed." Ben wiped the sweat from his forehead. It was only midmorning, and the registration for the Trials ended tomorrow at noon. They weren't far away, but he knew Greg would want to make an entrance.

"Fair enough."

"Best be getting a move on."

"We gonna make it today?" Jake asked.

"Not today. Boss will wanna make a big show, so we go in tomorrow."

"One more night outside," Jake said, reluctance in his voice.

"Just one."

Jake looked around, trying to distract himself from the ache in his arms from pulling the cart. There were no villages near the city, only the rough remains of the road that was to their right, the dirt track they walked along, and empty grasslands. Even the trees were gone, letting the lazy breeze waft past them. They couldn't sleep anywhere that wasn't exposed, but Jake knew Ben was right; they couldn't make it before sundown. Resigned to his duty, Jake bowed his head and ordered his limbs to quiet down.

Chris spent a day working on the car. Marty was nervous, nearly twitchy. He kept heckling Chris, trying to hurry him along. They had taken another Land Rover and removed the engine, Chris finally satisfied they were the same. After an oily morning the old one was out, placed on a wooden pallet so Marty could move it with one of the electric trucks. Chris lowered the new engine in, having changed some parts that Marty couldn't understand.

Leaving Chris to tinker and fettle the new engine, Marty headed for a wander around the bunker. It was massive, with deep tunnels into the rock. There were rooms full of food, of clothes, of equipment, all on metal shelves, all sealed and all labelled. There were metal containers with more equipment, small, one man cars with handlebars for controls, and strange looking boats made of black rubber. Wandering around the containers Marty realised he had never been in this far. He saw one that still had the red plastic seal on it.

Looking around he found some cutters and opened the container. He nearly laughed when he saw what was inside, but instead went for a battery and some fuel. Chris saw Marty gathering tools, but left him be. He knew the younger man had his own tasks and he trusted him. When you lived as they did, you had to trust your partner.

Dropping the flat bonnet Chris turned the engine over. It coughed and spluttered, but finally ran smoothly. With no smoke and no leaks underneath, Chris called for Marty.

"You finished?" Marty asked, appearing from the containers.

"Yeah. Bit of an arse, but I managed to get it running."

"Shame we don't have more of them cars."

"True. We need the weapons."

Marty grinned. "So you're sure that one's fixed?"

"It is. Now get over here so we can go."

"I wanna take my own transport, if I can." Marty said, diving into the containers.

"What transport?" Chris called back.

The clatter of a cold diesel engine echoed from the metal walls, and a shiny, unmarked Land Rover purred out. It was missing the weapons, but all the mounts were there.

"What about this one?" Marty asked. "I like the colour."

"Where the hell did you find that?" Chris said, open mouthed.

"In the back. You should have had a look for one."

"I did. How the hell?"

"Really, you are getting old." Marty smiled smugly, his boyish face looking even younger.

"I'll kick that smile off your face in a minute. Seriously, where did you find it?"

"One of the containers was still sealed. There's two in there."

Chris looked lost, so Marty showed him. Cursing under his breath Chris came out of the container. He gave Marty an irritated look, and went back to the cars.

"We take this one," he said, getting into the battered car. "I like *this* colour."

Marty held back his grin and helped load the car up.

"We heading out soon?" he asked Chris,

"Not tonight. Too late."

"We need to be there before midday tomorrow."

"How do you know?"

Marty reached into his back pocket and pulled out an old news roll. On the front page was the Trials, with the lunar cycle dating when they started.

"See? Half waxing moon, midday."

Chris looked at the roll. "Not gonna ask when you got this, and why you hid it. We can get there by then no worries. Be about ten hours' drive. Need a trailer for fuel and kit. So get me one."

Marty ran off for the small trailers the car could tow, while Chris looked over the roll. The reward for the winner was impressive, their own weight in precious metals. He had no need for that, but the title of Hunter Champion had it's appeal.

Tucking the roll into the net pouch behind the driver's seat, Chris went to chase Marty up with the trailer.

Chapter 14

It was early in the morning when Chris opened the metal door of the bunker. The mist still clung to the trees, but the warmth of the sun was felt already. It would be another hot day. Chris waved Marty out, waiting for the Land Rover and trailer to clear the door before he closed it. Sealing the bunker from the inside Chris left by the small side door. Once satisfied the bunker was secure he reset his traps and got into the car.

"I can drive you know," Marty said.

"I know. I taught you. But you ain't pulled a trailer before."

"You shoulda taught me that then."

Chris rolled his eyes. "Well, I will, one day. Just not this day. Where was this city of yours?"

Marty looked at the roll. "It says it's on the coast to the west. Large fishing city."

"I know it. It's not far from where I found you."

Marty started slightly. "You found me near a city?"

"Well, not too near the city. I figure your folks wandered from the coast and you were lost there."

"You didn't tell me that before."

"I never remembered it before. What's it matter?"

"Not much I guess." Marty slumped into silence as Chris drove the car in a random path to hide their tracks.

"Look, I know you wanna find out your past," Chris said. "And maybe you will when we get there. Just keep your mind on the job first."

"I always do."

"And if I can help you find yourself I will. You may speak with a strange accent, and have some random habits, but out here we are equal, and that means there is no difference between us. Age, history, future, they don't matter. Only us and our skill to survive and get the job done."

Marty stared at the woods as the trees thinned out. "How long until we get there?"

"Won't be long. There's a convoy road from there to the other cities. They ship a lot of food so the road is good."

"What do they send out?"

Chris swerved a tree stump and tried to pick his path. With the trailer it made driving and talking difficult. "Mostly fish. Usually salted and preserved. It's a delicacy to the rich fat city folks. They can't eat enough of it."

"You had any before?"

"Once. It was like salty tree bark."

"And that's a delicacy?" Marty asked.

"Apparently. They send a lot on the convoys. Always trucks rolling that way."

"And now old Precious has his electric factories he can make the stuff they need."

Chris nodded. "I wonder how old Precious is doing."

"I wonder about Piers."

"Yeah. Poor Compton. I bet he's still only a third level Officer."

"He heads their security now, don't he?" Marty asked.

"He did. That was a full cycle ago. You know what the cities are like. It's about power and money. You have the money you have the power. Mayor Precious may be out of office and the security forces disbanded."

"What about our weapons we lent them?"

Chris frowned. "I forgot about that. Best be going over there sometime. They said they could make more ammo, and we could do with topping up our reserves."

"We getting low?"

"Low? We have enough to wear out every gun we have easily. Just like to be sure."

Marty nodded. The trees had given way to open grasslands, and the car sped up. The cool breeze in their faces was a welcome relief to the heat that grew like a warming furnace. The sun still hovered well to their left, but once they hit the convoy road Chris turned right and they chased their shadow along the rough, patched road.

Chapter 15

The city did still hide behind it's impressive walls, but outside the gate a large tented village had been erected. Here, Hunters settled, ready for the Trials. It was laid out in a linear arrangement of individual tents, each with it's own screened-off space for training. Most of the men, and some women, already there, were settled in, exercising or talking. In the centre of the twin lines of tents was a large wooden cart carrying beer barrels with benches for the drinkers to sit at. Everyone else was here, enjoying the discounted beer brewed in the city.

The sound of banging metal stilled the drunken singing, and attracted those training out of their tents. They all looked down the road, watching the cart as it rolled slowly into the village. Two sweating men pulled the cart while one man, strong and handsome, stood on the top. He wore furs, but not the furs of a poor villager. These were elegant and clean, unmarked. They made his clean cut face look even smoother, his square chin more prominent. His arms and chest were bare, showing powerful muscles and a few scars.

In one hand he held a long, curved blade. In the other was a wicked serrated knife. His shoulder length auburn hair floated in the soft breeze as he stood in triumph. On his legs were cowhide trousers, patched but tough. His feet were covered in cowhide sandals. From his waist hung more blades, each reflecting the sun, making the onlookers blink and turn their heads from the sun's deflected glare.

"Greetings, Hunters," Greg said. "I am Flair Numlok, Champion of the Trials. You all can go home if you like. The winner stands before you."

"Yeah?" one Hunter called back. "You won already? I winner."

Greg clicked his tongue and the cart stopped by the speaker. Jake leant on the shaft and tried not to look too worn out. Ben smiled in anticipation of the coming display.

"I have," Greg said from the cart. "There is none who could best me."

"I bester than you," the man said.

Greg smiled and dropped to the floor. He stood before the man, who was a good foot shorter and half Greg's weight. He carried a battered wooden club, and had a dull stump of a knife in his tatty animal skin loincloth.

"You think you are better than me?" Greg asked with a polite friendly tone.

"Yar. I bester than you. You got muscles, I got brains, and I best here."

Greg smiled still, but one fist flashed like a piston, sending the man sprawling on the yellowing grass.

"I see," Greg said to the motionless man. "Clearly a tough adversary."

The crowd laughed with Greg as he leapt nimbly back onto the cart. Jake and Ben didn't wait for a signal, they pushed on the shafts of the cart. Once Greg had chosen the tent he wanted he clicked his tongue again. Dropping back to the hard packed dirt of the road he walked in and threw out the Hunter who was already there, throwing the man's meagre possessions after him. Ben and Jake managed with some effort to get the cart into the screened partition beside the tent, and rested under the shade.

"Water, and food of course," Greg said, striding from the tent.

Ben went with some silver slips for beer and food, while Jake filled a bucket from the communal well behind the beer cart. Greg stood by the entrance to his tent, letting the others see him. Looking over his competition he had little concern. Most used clubs or short blades. Some had hand held projectiles, mostly slings or the odd bow. Greg knew he would easily win the contest, so just stood in the sun and let the breeze ruffle his furs.

Ben signed them into the Trials, being the only one who could spell. Most of them had names written by the clerk, and thumbprints for signatures. It was nearly noon by the sundial placed near the beer cart, and Greg stood for the rest of the morning with a wooden flagon of beer in one hand, and the other resting on the hilt of his sword.

"You think we got this?" Jake asked Ben.

"Sure. The Boss can see this lot off. Mostly ignorant villagers anyway. They can't even read."

"I can't read," Jake added.

"True. But you didn't learn. They *can't* learn. There's a difference."

"Not to me."

"Whatever. We are gonna win this. Nobody's better than Greg."

Jake was about to reply when a grunt from Greg made them both jump. Joining their leader at the tent entrance they saw a crowd was forming in the road. Greg dropped his beer and pushed through, forcing his way to the front. Jake and Ben tagged along in his wake until they could see what the fuss was about.

In the distance something was coming down the road. At first it looked like a lone convoy truck, but as it drew closer it was clear it was a single vehicle, too small to be a convoy truck. It seemed to be moving by itself, as if it was rolling downhill. Unlike the convoy trucks, which were all black, this was dark green, with brown and black patches, making it hard to focus on. There were two men sat in the front, and a small cart attached to the back. Over the soft wind came the clatter of an engine.

"What is this wizardry?" Greg asked nobody in particular.

"The great Hunter," one of the crowd murmured.

"I am the Great Hunter," Greg said.

"This one hunts with fire and magic," the man said. "His sticks spit flames and everything drops down dead. He is a warlock, I'm sure of it."

"Bull," Greg said. "Fire sticks and magic. There is no such thing. Blades and brains, that kills out here, not magic."

The cart drew close, letting them all see the metal sticks on the roof and side, and the impressive menace the cart exuded. It stopped just short of the tented village, engine idling. The passenger got out, holding a black and green stick to his shoulder as if he was about to charge at them with it. The driver stood in his seat.

"I take it this is the Trials," the driver said.

"Registry is back here," someone called out.

"Thanks. You mind shifting?" The driver sat down while the younger man walked forwards, stick still in his shoulder, but pointing down. The crowd backed away, making space. The cart drove through them, stopping by the beer cart.

"What are you?" Greg asked, leading the crowd following after the cart.

"A Hunter, Chris Spencer's the name." Chris held out a hand.

Greg looked at it, then at Chris. "Spencer. You a warlock?"

"A what? I'm a Hunter. I'm here for the Trials."

"You both Hunters?"

"Yeah." Chris looked to Marty, but the man had wandered off. Cursing softly Chris drove the car beside the registry tent, making sure he could keep an eye on it. Once registered he was allocated a tent. He reversed the car and trailer inside and hung a piece of camouflaged cloth from the front, so Marty could find him. Then he checked over the car as usual and waited.

Chapter 16

Marty didn't reappear as the sun began to set. Feeling frustrated Chris decided to leave the car and find him. It seemed the Hunters kept to their own tents, with some local security force keeping an eye on them all. Walking to the massive city gates Chris saw they were closed. The smaller door in the gate was open, so he headed for that. Outside the door were four men in black and yellow uniforms. They held out their hands when Chris drew near.

"This area is off limits," one of the men said.

"I'm a Hunter," Chris replied.

"We know. That's why it's off limits. No one is allowed into the city unless they have a pass."

"What about this?" Chris asked, patting his pistol.

"That's not a pass, that's a threat."

"True. So, you gonna let me by?"

The man shook his head. "I am not allowed. Please go back to your tent."

"I would, but I think someone I know is inside the city and I wish to speak with them."

The man was about to reply when a voice from inside cut him off.

"Let that man pass," said the voice from behind the doorway. The security man frowned, but stood aside.

Chris smiled pleasantly and stepped through the door. He nearly walked back out again when he saw the speaker.

"Hello, Chris. Long time since we last met."

"Piers?" Chris said, smiling. "Is that really you?"

Piers nodded and they embraced.

"Old Precious is sponsoring this event, so they asked us to provide security for this," Piers explained to a confused looking Chris.

"So you ain't an Officer anymore?"

"Oh I am. I'm now a second level Officer of the Law. I got my own desk."

"Well done, I think," Chris said.

"So, where's Marty?"

"I've no idea. The little bugger went walkabout when we got here. Had a funny look on his face. You seen him go in?"

Piers shook his head. "Not on my watch, but I only started after midday."

"He would have been here before then." Chris looked over his shoulder. "Can you do me a favour?"

"For you? Anything."

"Can you get some of your men to watch the car? I need to find Marty."

Piers looked uncertain. "I can't really let you inside. Tell you what. I'll go and have a ferret around inside, and send him out. It's a crime for you guys to be inside."

"Precious thought the same."

"And Parks."

Chris shuddered. "That bugger. I really wanna kill him one day."

Piers looked surprised. "He's not dead yet?"

"No such luck. Anyway, go find Marty. Then we can all have a catch up."

Piers nodded and went to leave. Chris whistled, stopping him.

"What?" Piers asked.

"Nice to see you again, Officer Compton."

"You too, Mr Spencer." Piers waved Chris away and went through the inner gate. Chris watched him, then went back to his tent.

The old man hobbled from tent to tent, leaning heavily on his staff. The two younger men helped him, but kept a respectful distance. When they came to Chris' tent they stopped at the sight of the Land Rover. The old man laid a hand on the painted wing of the car.

"Can I help?" Chris asked, emerging from the back of the tent where he had been checking over his rifle.

One of the younger men stepped forwards. "I am Minister O'Keefe. I minister to the spiritual needs in the city. I am doing a series of visits to all our guests, attending to them as I can."

"Pleasure," Chris said, holding out a hand. O'Keefe hesitated, but shook the oily paw.

"Same. This is my assistant, Costello, and elder Glen." The other young man nodded at his name, and elder Glen tilted is head.

"What do they do?"

O'Keefe smiled. "Keep me from talking for hours. Costello is training to be a Minister. He will most likely replace me, or move onto another area. Elder Glen is our fount of knowledge. He knows the Holy book verse by verse."

"Impressive," Chris said. "How long does that take to learn?"

"All my life," Glen said in a dry rasp. "I never stop learning."

"Are you a man of faith in the reborn Saviour?" O'Keefe asked.

"Usually," Chris said. "In this job you have faith in three things; your eyes, your instincts, and your friends. For me, instincts are guided from a higher force."

The smile on O'Keefe's face showed the delight in what he heard. "How true, how true. So many live by their feelings without accepting why they feel them. You are almost wise enough to be an elder."

"Not old enough though," Glen wheezed.

Chris grinned and waved for them to sit. He had taken some of the equipment from the trailer, including some collapsible chairs, and with Costello's help they lowered Glen into one.

"Will you be there for our speech this Rest day?" O'Keefe asked once Glen was settled.

"I will try," Chris said. "To be fair I rarely get the chance to honour Rest day. Even in my village before I became a Hunter I couldn't often spare my duties on my land for Rest day."

"It's only once a week."

"True, but out there you need eight days in a week to survive."

O'Keefe shook his head, then nodded. "Fair enough."

"Forgive me, Minister," Chris said, "but you are not like most I meet of the cloth."

"How so?"

"Well, you are more sociable, more informal."

"More normal?" O'Keefe asked. "It's true, our branch of the faith do not walk the same ritual path of the others. We believe it's not where you praise, but how."

"How do you praise then?"

"Everywhere. In our hearts we sing and in our lives we shine." O'Keefe looked over the lines of weapons in the tent. "You are not like the other Hunters we have met either."

"I have been fortunate." Chris followed the Minister's gaze over his small arsenal. "One of the reasons I believe is lying before you now."

A scuffle outside the tent made them fall silent, looking to the entry flap. it was flung open and Marty came in.

"Where the hell you been?" Chris asked.

Marty just waved a dismissive hand and rolled into his hammock. Chris knew he wouldn't get any answers when Marty was in that mood, so he thanked O'Keefe for visiting and promised to try and make the Rest day service. Once they were alone Chris stood by the occupied hammock.

"I ain't talking about it," said the hammock. Chris watched for a moment, then went to his own. Let thinking men lie.

Chapter 17

The early morning sun was met with a chorus of snores from the tents. Some Hunters were up and exercising, jogging around the city, or training in open spaces. Chris slept late, having spent the night thinking. He woke to the sound of boiling water.

"You got a brew on?" he asked Marty without looking out of his sleeping bag.

"Always. Gotta take care of the old people."

"I'm not that old."

"Yeah, grandpa. Whatever. Anyway, got your brekkie all ready, some tea, and there's some shaving water left over too."

Chris polled out of his hammock and hopped over to Marty like a green worm.

"What's got you all motivated today?" Chris asked, unzipping the bag enough to release his hands. The sun was just rising but they could still see their breath in the early chill.

"Had some thinking to do, and this helps me think."

"Same here. So, what's your thinking resulted in?"

Marty sat on the collapsible chair and cradled his tea beaker in his hands. "About who I am."

"And?"

"I think I may know," Marty said slowly.

Chris leant back, eyes open fully now. Marty had no memory of his past ever since Chris had found him, with an impressive head wound, lying in the side of a road.

"I went for a walk into the city," Marty said, staring at his tea. "I saw all the market stalls, and I saw the fishing boats. I remember that time we went out of Laden and saw the boats on the river. It sparked something, and it did the same yesterday. So I went down to the boats and chatted to the fishermen. They were happy to talk, and even showed me the equipment they used."

Chris kept silent, knowing that Marty had sneaked into the city and to question any part of his story would most likely stop the flow. He needed to find his past, so he could regain his self awareness. Chris knew that once Marty did find his family he would probably leave to rejoin them, but that was a small price to pay for the young man who had helped Chris so much.

"We went out on the river," Marty continued to tell his tea. "I was only supposed to be watching, but something happened. I felt like I knew what I was doing, so I started making suggestions. They listened and followed my advice and it worked. We filled the boat with fish, and I even jumped on the kit, laying lines and nets better than they could. I was a fisherman before I was hurt, that I know now."

Sensing the monologue was at an end Chris spoke. "What's your next step?"

Marty nearly jumped when Chris spoke. "I heard tell that some of the fishing boats get caught in storms occasionally. The sea has land on the other side. Some of the bigger boats can make it if they carry enough food and water. Nobody goes over there as it's supposed to be like here. I think I was on a boat in a storm that was pulled over here. Or maybe my family came over with me and we moved inland. I don't know."

"You were a long way from the sea when I found you," Chris said.

"Exactly. If I was washed ashore and wandered around then I would be near the beach at least."

"You think your folks were captured? There are river raiders, remember?"

Marty nodded. "From Laden, yeah. That town, Gillam or whatever it was called."

"Gilliam, I remember that place. Met the Electrician there."

"True. He was a clever man."

"Very. You had a thing for fish there too." Chris drained his tea and grimaced as he slid out of his sleeping bag. Dressing quickly he shaved in the tepid water.

"They offered me a job with them," Marty said.

"With who"

"The fishermen. They said they'd never caught so many fish."

"What did you say back?"

Marty shrugged. "I said it was a fluke. They want me back today, but we got things to do."

"Not yet. Trials start tomorrow. All I gotta do is figure out the schedule, and how we do this."

"So we're doing the Trials then?"

"May as well, while we're here. By the way, we're banned from the city."

Marty laughed. "They know of us already?"

"Not so much. All Hunter's are banned."

"They come around and tell us all that?"

The tent flap opened and Piers came in.

"I told him," Piers said, straightening his uniform. "Can't have the riff raff in our lovely cities."

Marty stared, blinked, then leapt at Piers, giving him a warm embrace. They sat down and Piers brought them quickly up to date.

"So the mayor decided to make your ammunition, and we hope to be able to mass produce next cycle," Piers said. "The defence force is down to ten now, and the holes the dinos got in through have been fixed. Since we don't do much in the city anymore we ride the trucks, or patrol the walls and stand guard at the gates. It's a trifle dull since you guys left, to be fair."

"You still got the two cars we left?" Chris asked.

"Sure. One is used on perimeter patrols, the other is on standby. We converted that storehouse into a proper station now. We have bunks, an armoury, equipment shed and medical bay in there. Rather cosy for ten men."

"Nice," Marty said. "It was just a dusty old shed when we first got there."

"We put up a memorial slab for John outside," Piers said, his cheerful face clouding slightly. "It seemed right."

"We will come pay our respects there once this is over," Chris said, head bowed slightly.

"I gotta go," Piers said, standing. "It was great to see you both, and no going into the city. I don't wanna be the one who has to detain you."

"Good luck on that," Chris said, sparking laughter.

"Yeah, maybe. But let's not try to tempt fate." With a wave Piers left.

Marty cleaned up the beakers and waited for Chris to finish his breakfast pouch so he could clean the metal spoon. Once the kit was cleaned away Marty lingered by the car.

"Go on, sod off," Chris said, nearly pushing Marty out.

"You sure?"

"No, but go before I am."

Marty nodded a thanks and jogged off towards the gate to the city.

"You'll tell me sometime how you get in," Chris said to himself, then went back inside.

Marty was missing most of the next day too. Chris let him be alone. Instead, he went to see what Trials were.

"You'll find out," the bored sounding attendant at the information desk said, as if on automatic.

"Is that all you can say?" Chris asked.

"You'll find out," the man repeated with a ghost of a smile.

Realising the conversation was pointless Chris went to the beer cart. After a couple of incidents of Hunters investigating other people's tents guards were now posted all around the village, ensuring nobody went where they shouldn't. Chris waited in line for a beer and watched as that fancy Hunter stood on a table, making a dramatic speech.

In his furs and leathers he looked impressive, but too much show. Chris liked to get in and out without making too much noise. This guy looked like he did what he wanted. Maybe it worked for him, but it wasn't Chris' style. Sitting at a bench at the edge of the compound he watched the fancy Hunter, sipping his warm beer.

"Thought I'd find you out here," Piers said, sitting beside Chris.

"You want one?" he offered.

Piers shook his head. "Not while I'm working, which is for the next few days it seems."

"Fair enough. You know what these Trials are?"

"Not so much. I know there are some wooden targets to take down, and some live animals."

"Dinos?" Chris asked with concern.

"No, Sheep. There's a big area marked off near here. They have built stands and seats for the citizens of the city to come and watch."

"So we perform like a street corner entertainer?"

"Pretty much," Piers admitted. "To be fair I'm surprised you came."

"Why?"

"Didn't think this was your scene." Piers waved at the fancy Hunter.

"Who is that ass?"

Piers laughed. "That, don't you know, is Greg 'Flair' Numlok. The most elegant and showy Hunter around. The betting folk are putting him as favourite to win."

"Not me?"

"You, my old friend have no style."

"Who needs style?" Chris grunted.

"The people who pay good money to watch. They want flash, and excitement, and flair."

"So I need to put on furs and use a knife?"

"Just don't expect to win."

Chris put down his beer half drunk. "This is about who is the best Hunter, right?"

"Yes, and no. you see, the Mayor wants to add entertainment to this city's exports. The best in amusements, to give the people something to spend their new profits on as a result of the automation of manufacturing back home. This is the first step."

"Sounds dumb."

"It is, but people pay money for dumb."

"Not in the countryside," Chris said, looking into his beer.

"Not much money out there."

"So what do we win for these Trials then?"

"What ever you want." Piers lowered his voice. "The best prize is the only prize. You get to be the one who can claim to be the best Hunter, a load of cash from the city, and a place to live here if you want it."

"I already got that from your city."

"True. That's why I'm surprised you came here." Piers looked at the sky. "Gotta go back. Keep your eyes open, and watch your back, Boss."

"I always do."

Piers nodded and left, pausing to give Chris a long stare. He looked old and tired compared to Greg, but an old animal was harder to kill. Chris would be alright, Piers felt sorry for whoever tried to cross him.

Chapter 18

All the Hunters were gathered together the following evening. Marty had been away all day, so Chris stood alone with the others, his camouflaged clothing making him appear like a dead tree in a field of browns, furs and tanned skin. They stood by the beer cart, waiting. Finally a man came out of the city gates and stood on a small packing box.

"Greetings, Hunters," the man said through a speaking trumpet. "Thank you all for coming. These Trials will begin the day after tomorrow in the morning shortly after the sun has risen. There are many stages, each designed to test your skills, your accuracy, and your strength. To begin with there will be a target stage. This will show the power of your weapons, and your skill wielding them. The targets will be stationary wooden markers. Then follows another target stage with smaller targets. If you complete these stages then you will be allowed to begin the stalking stages. These will be against a variety of animals from sheep to rodents. This is to test your skills. The final stage will be against dangerous animals. For this we are using wild dogs. They will be wild, so only the best Hunters will be selected. From each stage Hunters who fall below the expected standard, or fail to complete a challenge, will be asked to leave. I suggest you prepare yourselves tomorrow for the Trials ahead, and good luck."

The man made a stiff short bow and left. The other Hunters dispersed, muttering to each other. Chris was about to leave when he saw two familiar figures. The taller man was big, with strong muscles. The other was similar, but slightly smaller. The shorter man saw Chris, nudging his companion, who smiled a lopsided grin and loped over.

"Spencer," the taller man said.

"Boulder. Impressed you made it." Chris returned the shoulder slap Boulder gave him.

"Trials for Hunters. We Hunters," Boulder said.

"Quite true. Hi, Chip," Chris said to Boulder's little brother.

"Spencer. You win?" Chip asked.

"Maybe, maybe not," Chris said, seeing Greg posing on the wooden crate.

"That guy?" Boulder said, half asking. "He no Hunter, he lady. Wears fur and cow skin like girl, not fight like man." Boulder touched his animal skin tunic, and the frayed cloth of Chris' jacket. "Not like us."

"Well, I don't know him," Chris admitted. "All I know is if he fights half as well as he talks he could win."

"He no win. We here." Chip patted his brother's shoulder. "Boulder beat him."

" Boulder beat me?" Chris asked with a hint of humour.

"Boulder smash you," Boulder said, smiling back.

"In that case I wish you good luck," Chris said, holding out a hand. Boulder looked at it, then slapped the hand gently. Chip did the same, and the two brothers went back to their tent.

Chris watched Greg as he paraded along the road outside the tents. He seemed cocky, even arrogant. You had to have some self assurance to be a Hunter, but this niggled Chris. Get in, do the job and leave. That was his work ethic. This Flair seemed to be all show as well as work. The Trials would show if he had any skill or not. Wondering where Marty had got too Chris headed back to his own tent.

"We gonna beat all of these losers," Ben said, filling his wooden flagon from the massive barrels on the beer cart. Jake already had his and was sat on a bench watching Greg.

"He deffo has a way with words," Jake admitted.

"It's more than that," said Ben, holding his beer in both hands. "Greg can beat anything. Look at that guy, in the green cloth." He pointed at Chris.

"The one with the fire sticks?"

"Yeah, him. He uses magic of whatever to kill. Greg uses his bare hands, and his brains. What's that guy gonna do when his magic runs out?"

"Get eaten?" Jake guessed.

"Exactly." Ben leant forwards, face over his drink. "You noticed there ain't any other magic Hunters about? Hm? That's because the magic's all run out. He's the last one, and he knows it."

"What about the young guy he runs with?" Jake asked, entranced into Ben's way of thinking.

"The foreigner? He's nothing. Some kid who lost his mind out there. Easily done."

"How do you know he's foreign?"

Ben sipped his beer. "His voice. Only ones who speak like that came over the water. I met some once. Their boat was caught in a storm and washed away. They spent days floating on the endless ocean. Finally they landed up near here."

"How did you know for sure they were from another land though?"

"The words, the voice, the boat. They looked like nothing you see around here."

Jake frowned. "We were brought up in a farming city. You know as much as I do about fishing boats."

"I know, alright. Greg told me. If you listed, you will learn things too."

Jake still looked unconvinced, but then Greg came over. He took Jake's beer and downed it in one long draw.

"This brew isn't too bad," Greg said. "We should have some fun with this lot. Maybe I should let them look good, before I come in and destroy them all."

"You can do it blindfolded, Boss," Ben said.

"I can, that's true. Maybe I should." Greg threw back his head and laughed. "If we have to stalk animals I can do it with my eyes shut. I once killed an entire dog pack in the dark."

Jake saw Greg was speaking loudly so everyone else near the beer cart could hear. It was beer and bragging time, and Greg would win this first round easily.

"Tell us about it," Ben said, playing his part in the act.

"I will," Greg said, dropping the empty flagon in front of Jake, who refilled it. "I was stalking this pack of wild dogs. There were more dogs than you have fingers and toes. More than even a money counter could count. It was like a river of barking dogs. I knew I couldn't beat them head on. I had to thin them out a bit."

Jake saw the crowd form, as they always did when Greg spoke. He could fill a space with bodies and keep them enthralled for hours. Jake kept refilling the flagon, to make sure Greg's throat didn't run dry.

"I moved along with the pack, watching where they went." Greg was in full flow, one foot on the bench, elbow on his knee. "I found the filthy pack's hole and waited until the dawn. Then I used my blades to gather dry grass, and a flint to light it with. I smoked them out of their hole and sliced each head clean off as they passed by me. Soon the entrance to their hole was blocked with bodies, so I cleared them away and went back to cutting. By the time the last one ran out I could hardly lift my arm."

Greg waved his right arm weakly, to emphasise the pain he had felt. "I couldn't move, I was exhausted, and the dry ground ran red with dog blood. Then I heard another. This was the pack leader. It saw me there, weak, tired, worn out. It bared it's teeth and charged. I couldn't hold my blade so I faced it barehanded. It leapt on me, knocking me to the ground. We rolled and fought amongst the bodies, it's own family. I held back those sharp teeth, the stinking breath washing over me. I felt my strength fail. I knew I had to do something before it killed me."

"What did you do?" asked a young man who had joined the large group listening in.

"Well, kid, I did all I could do. I knew I had a blade on my belt. with my good arm I held back the beast while using my tired arm to turn the blade upwards. Then I let the dog drop onto me. The blade ran through it's heart and I felt it's dying breath, the life fade from it's wild eyes, as it lay on top of me. I gathered my strength and pushed it away. It was a brave beast, so I made it's skin into my cloak." Greg shrugged his shoulders, letting everyone see the dog fur pelisse.

"Tell them about the monster pack," Ben said.

"The hairless monster people?" Greg asked, enjoying himself.

"The ones that stood on two legs like people, but had the body of a big chicken and the head of a snake."

"Well, that's an altogether different story," Greg said, taking another drink. "Even I don't know how I survived that pack."

Jake knew the night would be like this, so he just kept his head down and let Greg talk. The dog pack had been five animals, and the pelisse had been made from one they had found dead already, but Greg was known for his flair in storytelling, and this was his story, so Jake let him tell it.

Chapter 19

Chris spent the evening checking the weapons on the car. He knew they were fine, but he needed something to distract him. He considered joining some of the others who went for a run around the city walls, but decided against it. He knew Marty would be coming back at sometime and he wanted to be there. His stomach rumbled but Chris didn't eat. They always ate together, and he would wait. He'd been without food before, he could manage now.

It was well past sun fall when Marty came in. He stank of fish.

"Where you been?" Chris asked.

"Out."

"All day?"

Marty looked Chris up and down. "So? What the problem?"

"You know these Trials you were so keen to do?"

Marty shrugged. The difference in him was solid, like he had changed his body. He looked more alert, stronger. "I was doing things."

"You wanna talk about it?" Chris tried to keep his voice soft, but the irritation crept in.

"Not really."

"You gonna be here tomorrow?"

Marty looked at the cold stove and lit it. "What's happening tomorrow?"

"Nothing. Trials start day after."

"Then I'll be here the day after."

"Will you?"

Marty's shoulders sagged. "I know who I am now." His voice was weak, faltering.

"Really? You know your past finally?"

"Not all of it," Marty said, sitting by the stove. The blue and yellow flame cast mad shadows on his young features. He looked older.

"How much do you know now?"

"I know I came from over the water. I know I used to fish, and my father did too."

Chris sat on the dry dirt opposite Marty. "You know what happened to him?"

"No. The local fishermen say they knew of a group of ships that were cast adrift in a big storm and ran aground near here. Some of them settled in the city. They fish now. I was talking with another crew when one of them recognised me."

"They knew you?" Chris asked, eager. This could have been the breakthrough Marty needed.

"They said they knew of my father, and me. They didn't really know me well, but they knew my face. They said we came from a town over the water. They described it. It's nothing like here."

"What's different."

"No walls. The houses are made of wood. They live in towns with normal lives. No dinos."

Chris half smiled. "That sounds a little dull."

"It's how they live, how I used to live."

"You wanna go back there?"

Marty shrugged. "Maybe. One day perhaps. They say there's no way to cross the waters, and only to lucky make it over."

"So, if your boat made it, where is your dad?"

"They didn't know. The best guess they could offer is we went to settle north of here and ended up lost. Finally we were separated. Then you found me."

"Or you were attacked."

"Possible," Marty nodded.

"Hey," Chris said with sympathy. "This is amazing. You're a big step closer to knowing who you are."

"Yeah." Marty didn't sound convinced.

"What's wrong?"

"I thought I'd feel different, but I don't. I asked where our boat was, but they said we took it with us. Why would we leave the boat?"

"Maybe something chased you? Plenty out there to make you run."

Marty nodded, waiting for a convoy to pass their tent. Being beside the main road was easy for access, but it made it hard to speak when the big trucks thundered past. The thick smoke was choking.

"You say my fumes are bad," Chris said.

"Especially after beans," Marty nodded, eyes streaming from the smoke.

Chris smiled, glad the old Marty was back. "You wanna go back into the city tomorrow then go. I can hold it down here. Then we do the Trials the day after."

"You sure?"

"Go on and get some sleep. And you can show me how you get inside the city sometime too."

"As if you couldn't guess," Marty said, standing. He stopped by Chris, laying a hand gently on the older man's shoulder, then went to bed.

"And have a wash next time. You stink of fish." Chris smiled sadly and put some water on to boil. Taking a food pouch from the car he looked up at the stars. It was still warm and he knew it would stay that way. Soon he may be looking at those stars all alone, and the thought scared him. If Marty did go back over the water Chris was tempted to join him. Maybe a new start would help them both.

The following morning Chris went out and watched the other Hunters. At best guess there were about fifteen different groups. Some were lone men, wild and suspicious. Others, Like Greg, had a group with them. Most seemed to be in pairs. He walked the dirt road that led from the city gate and thought. Passing the beer cart he saw some of the Hunters were already draining one of the big barrels. They argued and bickered until Piers and his security force had to step in. Piers himself nodded a greeting to Chris whilst arguing physically with a drunken man.

Chris knew his car was safe, so he left the tented village and headed for the Trials arena. Here a large roped off section as large as a village held wooden targets. Around one half of the rough circle were stands so people could sit and watch. Some carpenters were working on the supports and ignored Chris as he looked over the arrangements. His attention was more attracted by the targets.

Each was about man sized, made of thick wood. They stood in a line in a single row of four. Others lay nearby, waiting to be fixed to the posts sunk into the dry, hard soil. On each oval target was a red paint mark. Around this was a blue mark, larger like a ring. And a green ring filled half the target. The rest was unpainted. Chris fingered the wood. It was tough, decent building lumber.

"You cheating here?" a voice said.

Chris spun around, one hand on his holster. He stopped when he saw Greg.

"You have the reactions of a Hunter," Greg said, cocking his head and smiling. "I wonder if you could be my greatest opponent."

"Maybe. We will see tomorrow."

Greg laughed. "You hear that?" he asked, nodding towards the tents. The sound of drunken singing and fighting mixed with the orders for calm on the warm air. "That's the sound of chaos. Those fools don't know what it means to be a champion, a winner."

Chris kept silent as Greg walked around him slowly.

"You see," continued Greg, pacing. "You and me, we are similar. We both want to do the job, we both get it done, and we both live. For you, the appeal is in your past. Yes, I know about you,

Spencer. You have a noble cause to fight. For me, I like the attention."

"You feel better about your own weaknesses," Chris said, tetchy about the mention of his own past.

Greg feigned hurt. "I have no weaknesses. I have my skills, and my abilities. I know I can do this, and I will do this. Do the job. Same as you. Only I will do it with style. That's what they want here. Style. Give them a show."

"What makes you think style matters?"

"Open your eyes, old man," greg said, waving at the stands. "Do you think they would build such a thing if nobody would want to watch? Why was good timber used on a bunch of savage men? This is a show, and that is what they need. You have a skill, an ability they could only dream about. Don't waste it here."

Chris smiled, putting Greg off his stride.

"You think I should leave?" Chris asked.

"You should. This is no place for you. Out there, in the wild, where nobody is watching. That is your place. Leave the showground to those who can entertain."

"Thank you," Chris said.

"For what?"

"For showing me you are scared of losing to me. Now I know your weaknesses and how to win."

Without waiting for a reply Chris turned and headed back to the village. He passed the workmen, who had paused in the midday heat to watch the two men. They seemed disappointed there wasn't a fight. Back at the tents Chris saw some of the men were still fighting, and waded in. Once the brawl had broken up a dirty and tired Piers thanked Chris. Waving a farewell Chris headed back to his tent. It was getting hot, and inside the thick canvass it was too warm to sit so he took a water bottle and sat in the weak breeze outside, watching everyone pass.

Marty had managed to find an old drain that allowed him to get inside the city. He knew that Chris would follow, so he hid some large pebbles in the thick dust that half filled the drain. Inside the walls Marty used an old boating cloak to hide his clothes while he headed for the docks. The city held its boats in a large crescent dock, with wooden jetties floating on the water. From these the fishermen could check their equipment and ready their boats. The base of the crescent was blocked by the city, but the narrow southern end was barred by huge gates that were half submerged in the water. Once opened these gates allowed the boats to leave.

Near the gates was the unloading dock. Here each boat lined up to have their catch weighed, their ledgers filled, and their pay given before they moored up at their own bay. Marty ignored this area as it was busy and held a permanent security presence. Instead he headed for the bay he knew well. Passing the stalls selling both fish and fishing equipment Marty ignored the calls from the sellers. Some even sold women for a short period. This was harder for Marty to ignore, but he did it. His past mysteries called more than his present urges.

Stepping onto the floating pontoon jetty Marty waved at the fishermen, who waved at him to hurry up. The tide was going out and most of the other boats were already raising their single sails and heading for the gates and the open sea. Marty jogged on the unsteady platform, knowing they would wait, but he wanted to make it look like he was making an effort to not delay them anymore.

Chris slithered through the drain, his wider build making it harder to fit. The big stones in the dirt made it harder to get through. He saw the stands at the same time he smelt the salt of the sea and the rotten stink of dirty water. The city dumped its waste into the sea and in the crescent dock it stayed, waiting for the tide. Knowing his clothes stood out Chris tried to use the stalls as cover while he looked for Marty. He knew the younger man would hide himself, but Chris wanted to know where he went.

Hiding behind a stall loaded with wooden hooks for hanging fish Chris saw a small boat row away from the nearly empty docks. Its thin mast held a limp sail of patched cloth, but the man in the back in a boater's cloak was what caught his eye. Marty was fishing. That's why he was so distracted. Satisfied Marty was safe Chris turned to go back. He weaved through the stalls until a woman's scream, cut short, stopped him. Hand on his holster he went after the sound.

A podgy man in decent cloth was almost glowing in rage. Behind him several young women cowered away. One lay sobbing on the floor.

"Get up, you stupid girl," the man said, lifting a wooden paddle and dropping it hard onto her exposed shoulders. The sound made the other girls jump in fear. "I said get up!"

The paddle rose again, but stopped. The man looked in surprise at his wrist, now clamped in Chris' hand.

"What you think you're doing?" he asked Chris, who smiled.

"I was about to ask you the same thing." Chris kept his grip on the man's wrist even as he tried to wriggle free.

"This is none of your business. This is a matter between myself and my staff," the man said.

"I think you are doing something you shouldn't to this young lady, and for that I should stop you."

The man laughed. "You know what she is?"

"A woman, with a mouth and mind of her own," Chris said, straight faced.

"She's my property. Her father sold her to me to repay his debts. That makes her mine, and if I say she spends her time satisfying the men of this city, then that is what she will do."

"Do you want to do that?" Chris asked the girl.

"It doesn't matter what she wants," the man said, aware a crowd was forming.

"I think it does. She has a mouth, she can speak for herself."

"Her mouth, like the rest of her, is my property," the man insisted. He opened his mouth to speak, but only let out a soft moan as the grip on his wrist tightened.

"I think you have beaten these poor ladies enough," Chris said.

"What makes you think that?" the man asked in a strained voice.

"Me, that's what. Nobody is a slave to anyone."

"The law here says I can own slaves," the man said. "So I own slaves. They owe me money, and you can't do anything about it."

Chris smiled, then released the man's hand. As the slave owner rubbed his wrist he turned to face Chris, then stopped, wide eyed. Chris had braced his legs and with a single motion he lifted the fat man onto his shoulders. He ignored the man's protests and the fists that pounded on his back. Instead he strode with confidence until he reached the water's edge. With a shrug he tipped the man into the water.

"How much does she owe you?" chris asked the man.

"You'll pay for this," came the damp reply as the man tried to reach one of the many ladders fixed to the dock wall.

"How much?"

The man shook his head and climbed the ladder. As he reached the top Chris placed one booted foot on the wet head, pushing it back gently but firmly.

"How much does she owe you?" Chris said.

"Three discs of metal," the man replied, shaking the foot off.

Chris fished inside his camouflaged shirt for the discs and gave them to the man. At the same time he pushed him back into the water.

"Consider the debt paid," Chris said. Walking back to the girl he helped her to her feet. As he led her towards the gates he saw Minister O'Keefe, who nodded.

Chapter 20

Piers let Chris through with the girl. He knew not to ask questions. The fat man had lodged his protest, but Piers simply replied it was a civil matter and the offender was someone who was from the city, as all Hunters were banned from entering.

Taking her gently back to his tent Chris sat the girl down and gave her some water. Setting the stove to heat some food he sat opposite.

"Do you want to have me now, or after we eat?" the girl asked with a slight tremble in her voice.

"I don't intend to have you at all," Chris replied. He smiled when she looked puzzled. "I didn't take you out of there for my own pleasure."

"Then why did you?"

"Because nobody deserves to be treated like that."

The girl smiled slightly, making her dirty and tired face childlike. "What makes you think I didn't deserve it?"

"People who accept their guilt accept their punishment. You didn't seem accepting."

"True, I suppose. So why am I here?"

"So you can be safe."

"From whom?"

Chris dropped a pouch in the bubbling water. "Them, that man who beat you, everyone."

"What about you?"

"I wanna be safe from them too."

She laughed, the age and pain falling from her face like a mask. "I mean am I safe from you?"

"Sure. Maybe not Marty though."

"Who's Marty?" she asked.

"You'll see. Who are you anyway?"

"Claire. Claire Shaw."

"Chris Spencer," Chris said, offering a hand. Claire took it gently, in case his grip hurt.

"So, Chris, what do you do beside rescuing women?"

"I'm here for the Trials."

"A Hunter?" she asked, eyes suddenly intense.

"Thought the clothes gave it away."

"Sorry, it's just I was told tale of you men."

Chris took the pouch out and checked it was hot before handing it over. "There's plenty of us out here."

"I heard that too," Clair replied, gingerly poking her long tongue into the pouch.

"So how come you never met any of us?"

Claire tasted the stew in the pouch, her eyes half closing in pleasure. "How does your food taste so good?"

"Really? I always thought it was a bit bland." Chris smiled his lopsided grim.

"Bland? After stale bread and goat's milk this is heaven."

"Plenty of heaven in the back of the car."

Claire looked at the old Land Rover. "What is that?"

"My car. So how come you never came out the city, never saw the Hunters you heard about."

"I'm not allowed. I never leave the city."

"Why?"

Claire put down the half empty pouch and sighed. "My father was a fisherman. His boat was damaged in the docks. Never happens, but his was. He was forced to sell it to pay his debts. When that wasn't enough I was sold. I think Selby did the damage because he wanted me in his little harem."

"Selby?" Chris asked.

"The fat man you saved me from. He buys all the pretty girls for pleasure, and the boys for security. We don't perform, we get beaten."

"And you didn't want to perform," Chris said.

"No, I didn't," Claire replied, shaking her head. "I don't believe in that sort of thing. I wanted to wait until I was joined."

"Wanted?"

Shadow passed over Claire's face. "I was forced," she said, her head bowed, long dark hair hiding her face. Chris didn't press. Instead he stood and looked at his hammock.

"You ever slept in one of these?" he asked.

Claire looked up with damp cheeks. "No. I always had to sleep on the floor. Girls like me don't get comfy beds, save for when we have customers of course."

Chris shrugged and pulled a sleeping bag and some blankets from the back of the car. Laying them out in a corner away from the entrance he made a rough bed.

"You can sleep here, if you like. As long as we are here, you can stay with us."

Claire looked ready to cry, her face creased in emotion. "Really?"

"Really. You're safe here, at least from me anyway."

"Marty?"

Chris nodded. "I'll warn the little bugger. He'd make a good husband for someone, but they'd have to be pretty harsh to control him."

"I don't know how to thank you."

"Just rest and regain your strength. Then you can decide on your future. Until then, consider yourself under my personal protection." Chris made sure Claire was settled in the bed, then went outside. In the warm sun he waited, leaving her in peace. She would be tired and confused, so the time alone would help her accept what had happened. Unsurprisingly Piers arrived with Selby, who pointed out Chris.

"That's the culprit," Selby said.

"Mr Spencer," Piers began, sounding official.

"Officer Compton," Chris replied. Both men struggled to keep a straight face. Fortunately Selby was too angry to notice.

"I have a report that a man matching your description assaulted this gentleman, by which he was thrown into the water and hit with a money purse," Piers said.

"A money purse? Did it contain money?"

"It did."

Chris clenched his teeth to stop the laughter, which Selby saw as anger. "If someone threw a money purse containing money at me I would not mind getting a little wet."

"This gentleman also claims you stole some property from him," Piers managed with a tremble. Both knew they couldn't hold in the hysterics for long.

"Then I suggest this gentleman looks elsewhere," Chris said. "I only have what I came with, and no other possessions."

"I will continue my enquiries," Piers said to Selby, who left. Once the fat man was out of sight both men collapsed in fits of laughter.

"Did it contain money?" Piers said, sparking fresh tears.

"I wouldn't mind getting a bit wet," Chris added, sending them both rolling on the dirt floor again.

"What's going on out here?" Claire asked. When she saw Piers she gasped, fearful the Law had come to take her back. When she saw he was laughing with Chris she looked puzzled, but giggled with them.

"Hello there, stolen property," Chris said to Claire, sending a slowly rising Piers back to his knees.

"Hello," Claire said, still bemused.

"Piers," Chris called, trying to get the man to stand. "Piers, come on. Be professional."

They stopped laughing and looked at each other, then burst into tears again. Chris had to help Piers inside where they both finally calmed down.

"Claire Shaw, this is my old friend Officer Piers Compton," Chris said, wiping his eyes.

"Pleasure," Piers said. "I take it this is his 'stolen' property?"

"True," Chris said. "I'm a bad bad boy."

"Why are you here, Ms Shaw?"

"Chris saved me," Claire said.

"He does a lot of that," Piers said, rolling his eyes when Chris smiled smugly.

"A lot of what?" Marty asked, coming into the tent. He saw Claire and looked both shocked and amused at the same time.

"Marty, you're back early," Chris said.

"Clearly. You having some friends over without me?" he asked.

"Not so much," Chris admitted. "This is Claire Shaw. I found some nasty little piece of work in the city selling her off to men for coin. I stopped him."

"Really?" Marty stripped his shirt off, knowing Claire would be watching. His newly toned physique caught her attention. "And what you gonna do with her now you saved her?"

"Whatever she wants," Chris said. "She's free."

"I'm free?" Claire asked, still staring at Marty.

"You are. Go and live your life."

"Where?"

Chris opened his mouth then closed it. "No idea. I imagine that will take some time to figure out."

"You wanna help us we could do with some jobs doing around here," Marty said, sniffing a shirt.

"I can do that," Claire offered.

"You're not doing his chores," Chris said.

"Just the laundry and dishes," Marty said.

"That's all you do," Chris replied.

"True, but we got these Trials coming up tomorrow. Why I'm back early."

Piers coughed. "Best not be going back into the city though, just in case Selby tries anything. Out here I can keep them away. In there I have no powers."

"Agreed," Chris said. "Marty, sorry but you're staying out here."

"Good luck with that," Marty said, taking another shirt and walking out.

"He been a bit weird lately?" Piers asked.

"No more than normal," Chris replied. "Think it's his family. Someone in there knows them and he wants to find out who they were."

"He's found his family?" Piers asked, suddenly animated.

"Not so much, but he's closer now than he used to be."

Claire watched them talk and slowly drifted to the car. Seeing the pile of musty clothes in a canvas sack in the back she pulled it out and headed for the stream. She was determined to repay her protector, and doing some odd jobs was far better than the life she'd been saved from.

Chapter 21

Early the following morning Chris woke and made himself ready. Marty was still in his hammock so Chris left him sleep. He also left Claire in her bed nest in the corner. Looking outside Chris saw the road was filling up with the early risers. Some were jogging, others practicing with wooden poles. Chris ignored them and went back inside to check the car over.

One of the pieces of equipment Chris found most useful was the belts. This could have pouches added or removed depending on what you needed. He took his own belt and stripped it down to the belt and yoke. Then he added two ammunition pouches to the front, a water pouch each side, and an equipment pouch at the back. In the ammo pouches he emptied, checked and refilled two magazines per pouch. His water bottles he filled from the well, and in the final pouch he put some food. Satisfied it was secure and comfortable he moved on to his rifle. Today was supposed to be a parade of competitors, and more of a ceremony, but Chris wanted to be ready just in case. There shouldn't be anything dangerous near the city, but Chris wasn't the type to take chances.

"You getting ready now?" Marty yawned from behind. He was only wearing his green under-shorts and boots.

"Yeah. You should too, after a wash, shave and you get dressed."

"I can do that after I prep."

"Nope," Chris said, shaking his head. "We have delicate eyes here." He nodded to Claire, who snored softly.

"Meh," Marty said, but took the wooden bucket and went to the well. Chris watched him go, then went back to stripping his rifle.

"You're gonna wear that out just cleaning it," Marty said, damp from his wash. He lit the small stove and put some water on to boil.

"At least I know it's fine. You putting some brekkie on?"

"Can do. Wanna shave after."

"Good. We're on show today so gotta look half civilised."

"Since when did you care about looking good?" Marty asked, flicking through the food sack.

"I get the feeling this is not only about being good."

"How so?"

Chris looked over the parts of his rifle laid out on the flat bonnet of the Land Rover. "They have viewing stands for people to watch, and a big circle for us to work in."

"You go snooping?" Marty mused, dropping two pouches into the steaming water.

"Naturally. There's just some wooden boards for us to aim at. Decent wood too."

"Spent some coin on us then."

"Seems so," Chris agreed.

Marty poked the pouches with a stick while Chris finished reassembling his rifle. The loud click as he released the spring tension woke Claire.

"Is it morning already?" she asked, half asleep.

"Afternoon," Marty said.

Claire's eyes went wide. "Afternoon? Already? How could I sleep so long."

Chris threw an oily rag at the giggling young man. "It's early morning. We're just getting ready for this daft parade thing."

"Oh, ok. Do you want me to cook for you?"

"Already on it," Marty said, adding another pouch to the water.

"What about bathing you?"

"Done," Chris said.

"Oh." Claire looked a little deflated, so Chris asked if she could help clear all the leaf litter from the tent. It didn't really need doing, but he knew a busy person was a happy person, and Claire needed to feel like she was useful.

Marty dressed and did his own equipment belt, Chris checked Marty's rifle while the younger man got ready. A loud trumpet horn sounded from the gates, calling them all out. Claire hung close to Chris, but he told her to stay with the car. The two men stepped out into the harsh early morning sun and followed the shuffling swarm of Hunters as they walked towards the arena.

Greg was at the front, standing proudly on his cart while Ben and Jake pulled him. The other Hunters followed behind, some silent, some muttering about getting up early. They neared the arena and could hear the sound of a large crowd ahead. Some officials in a dark uniform stopped them. Chris saw Piers among them. They arranged the Hunters in single groups and let them go one at a time. As they entered the arena the people banged sticks together as a man on a platform announced each Hunter through a speaking trumpet.

When it came to be his turn Chris felt nervous. Normally he was used to dealing with groups of people, but this was different. Here they wanted to see action, danger, excitement. The biggest shock that he and Marty could give would be firing a weapon into the air, but that was a waste of ammunition. Instead they walked side by side into the arena.

"Christopher Spencer, and Martin Fritz-Herbert," the announcer said.

Chris felt he should do something, but he couldn't think what. Marty on the other hand knew how to play up to the crowd, all those women he had bedded taught him how to pose. He nudged Chris and then knelt with his rifle raised, as if sighting a target. Chris felt foolish, but did the same, facing in the opposite direction. The crowd seemed to like this, banging their sticks again. Satisfied they had made an impression Marty stood and waved. Chris did the same, feeling clumsy. They walked out the other side and another Hunter walked into the arena.

"That sucked," Chris said.

"I always said you had no style," Marty replied with a smile.

"I kill the buggers. How much flair do I need?"

"You need flair here, Spencer," Greg said, striding through the growing group. "This is not your show. I did say that before."

"True, but that don't mean I'm out already."

"Go home, old man. Before you make a fool of yourself."

Chris tensed, wanting to retort. Instead he stared at Greg, then turned and left. Marty sneered at Greg, then followed.

"What's wrong?" Marty asked when Chris stopped. They watched the arena as the announcer explained the trials.

"Just hate people who live off fame over skill."

"He can do the job. If you ain't good you ain't alive, you know that."

"I know. Just he grates on something I forgot I had. Something about him makes me want to drop him."

Marty laughed. "I agree, but how many have we had like that in the past? This world is full of people like him. Just forget it."

Chris sighed. He'd been foolish, and Marty had been the sensible one for a change. That rattled him even more.

"You're right, Marty. I'm sorry. They want a show? This bunch of children can wave their clubs and bows. We will show them how deadly we are. That's more entertaining."

Marty beamed and throwing an arm around Chris' shoulders they walked back to the group.

Chapter 22

The next day the list of Hunters went up on the side of an empty beer barrel. Beside each were several boxes. They were told that they went in the order of their names. As not all of the Hunters could read it was suggested they remembered who went before them so they knew. The Trials began at midday, so the Hunters took the time to make themselves ready.

Marty had vanished that morning again, but came back in time to see Chris getting dressed. Claire was helping him.

"I always knew he was getting too old to get dressed," Marty said as he came in. Chris waved a hand dismissively at the younger man's back, and shrugged Claire off. Marty stripped his shirt off, letting Claire see his newly toned figure, then took a new one from the top of a pile. He sniffed it and smiled.

"She cleaned everything," Chris said.

"I owe you men," Claire said.

"Not really, but thanks," Marty said, pulling the shirt on and fumbling with the buttons. Claire smiled and came closer to help.

"He doesn't need help putting a shirt on," said Chris. "Usually the girls help him take one off though."

Marty stuck out his tongue, but noticed Claire stepped back.

"I can manage," Marty said. "When we on?"

"When do you think?" Chris replied from the car.

"After Greg?"

"Before. That worm wiggled it so his name is last."

"Grand finale?" Marty asked, joining Chris.

"Probably. I'm just gonna go in and do what they ask."

They checked their weapons and equipment, said their farewells to Claire, and left.

It was hot outside in the sun. Their clean clothes were already damp from sweat. Chris sent Marty to find a well so they could refill their bottles, but the only one was back at the tents. Chris waited impatiently for him to return. The other Hunters sat in the shade and waited, each almost in a line so they knew who was before them. One sat too close to another, who waved a sharpened stick at him.

"You keep that away," the other man said.

"You move, or stick will stick you," said the first. Piers was on duty with his men, so they broke up the squabble before it grew. The arena was hidden from them behind a screen, but some watched through the thick canvas. Marty joined in and reported that they had three wooden boards to attack as accurately as possible.

"Sounds easy enough," Chris said.

"Like taking fruit from a child," Marty agreed.

"Being good isn't enough," Greg said, having snuck up behind them. "You need style, flair, and skill."

"And *you* need to not be sneaking up around folks," Chris said.

"Did I scare you amateurs?" Greg asked with open mocking.

"No," Chris replied. "But you nearly lost your nuts."

Greg looked down and saw Chris had his pistol muzzle buried in Greg's furs.

"I take your point. You are on before me. This will be an interesting display, but I suggest you watch mine closely."

"I take your point," Chris said. "Now sod off with it."

Greg nodded and left. Chris remoistened is pistol.

"You don't like him much," Marty said, watching Greg as he strutted around the other Hunters.

"He likes to show off. Grates a nerve."

"Why?"

"He's like some raider leader, covered in fancy furs and acting like he is best. All he needs is a banner or something and he could be a raider."

"He's harmless, I hope."

Chris grunted, but shook himself off when the man before them stood and ambled around the screen.

"Looks like we're next," Chris said, checking his rifle.

"How we doing this?"

"I think we go in, nod and bow to the crowd, then stand at the start line and just use the rifles on the targets. They fall down if you hit them?"

Marty nodded. "Don't know if it's done by itself, or if someone else dies it, but when they do you move on."

"Plan." Chris saw the uniformed man waving them over and checked his magazine. "Show time."

They walked side by side, rifles over their shoulders, into the roped off arena. Chris felt his heart pound. There were hundreds of people watching. The stands had been finished overnight and they now nearly encircled the arena. Marty coughed and half nodded at the black screened box in the centre of the stands. There stood an Internal Affairs agent with a man who was possibly the mayor.

Staying together they marched to the box, nodded to the mayor and gave a short, stiff bow. Then they did the same to their left and right. Another uniform stood by the start line. Standing by the wooden pole that marked the beginning Chris looked over the targets. The wooden boards had marks from the other Hunters, but few holes.

"Rifles, load," Chris said softly. Both men took their rifles from their shoulders at the same time, cocked them, and lifted them to their shoulders, ready to fire.

"Aim," Chris said. Marty lined up his sights on the board before them. They both stood with one leg back, one forwards, rifles held unwavering in their hands.

"Fire," Chris hissed. The rifles bucked, making the crowd jump. In the sudden silence afterwards only a baby's cries split the peace. The first board rocked, but stayed upright. Murmurs of disapproval began to flow from the crowd. They fired again and the board just rocked again.

"What we do?" Marty hissed, rifle still raised.

"Sod it. Blow the bugger to hell." They flicked the lever on their weapons to full automatic and emptied their magazines into the first board. The smoke cleared and the two ragged halves slowly peeled apart. The uniform coughed politely and ushered them to the next one. Reloading with fresh magazines they decimated the next board. The crowd remained silent, so Chris bit his lip and waved Marty back.

Ignoring the uniform who tried to move them along Chris instead walked away. Stopping near the opposite end of the arena he checked the fat tube under his rifle.

"You sure that's a good idea?" Marty asked.

"Probably not, but I ain't letting Greg beat us." Chris took the other trigger that lay before the magazine and lined up the flip up sights. With a sly smile he fired.

The puff of gas hid him from the crowds, but the explosion as the bomb blew the target to pieces made them gasp. Some women screamed and collapsed. The men murmured about the insult. The uniform looked in shock from Chris to the target. With a half smile of admiration he waved them out of the arena while the crowds banged their sticks without enthusiasm. Greg walked in after they had left and held up his arms, showing his strength. He even helped clear up the debris and reset the new targets.

That night, after all the Hunters had finished drinking and finally fallen asleep, Piers wandered the tented village. He saw most of the men lying drunk on the floor, snoring loudly. Some had found women to hold, but most were alone in the dirt. As he passed around the beer cart he saw movement. Drawn like a moth to a flame he moved swiftly, but with caution, using the techniques he had learnt from Chris when they had worked in the big city. When he caught up with the darting figure he held back, close enough to hear the conversation held between his target and some men who looked familiar.

"Today went well?" asked the man Piers had followed. He sounded hopeful.

"Today went well," confirmed the taller of the other three men. Piers realised it was the city mayor. "They gave a show that more than satisfied the crowds."

"Except one," said a short, round looking man.

"Except one," the mayor nodded. "I think Spencer should be removed."

"He did what was asked," the third pointed out.

"True, but he was dull, unexciting," the fourth man said. He was still breathing heavily from his fast walk. "I watched him. He hit the targets perfectly, but he did it like a butcher cuts meat. he was precise, but no show."

"Not like Numlok," the dumpy man said. "He had flair."

"He is Flair," the mayor said. "He is our winner I think, if he keeps up his performance."

"I can't see a reason why he shouldn't," the fat man said. "I hear the bet-makers are putting a certified win on Flair Numlok."

"That won't help us to earn off the bets," the fourth man said with more concern.

"True, but think of how we will feel once we have the prize Hunter in our grasp?" The mayor waved a hand. "Remove Spencer, and add a few of the poor performers."

"He did that flash and bang show though," the third man mused. "I liked that."

"Made a mess of the whole arena," the fat man moaned.

"And Numlok helped clear it up. A champion if I ever saw one." The mayor wafted his hand again and walked away. The fat man left with the third, leaving the one Piers had followed. This man looked almost confused, then he shrugged and left. Piers considered following him, but decided to go see Chris instead.

Chapter 23

Chris woke early. Piers had told him the night before that the organisers had planned to remove him from the event and he wanted to be there when the names were updated. Only a couple of Hunters were at the board by the beer cart when the official came out with the rolled up list. He used stubby nails to hold it in place, then left. The others looked quizzically at the paper, but Chris saw his name right at the bottom. It had a large X next to it.

"Saw that coming," a voice behind said. Chris turned to see Numlok leaning against the cart.

"Saw what?"

"Your losing. I told you, this isn't your scene." Greg stood up and walked to the board. His own name was on the top of the list.

"See? You need style, not accuracy to win something like this."

Chris sneered and turned away.

"You may be the better Hunter," Greg said to Chris' back. "But I'm the better showman. That is what makes a winner."

Chris went to the gate and waited until the officials came out.

"Can I help?" one asked. Chris recognised him from the registration table.

"Yes. I'm Chris Spencer."

"I'm aware of who you are," the short fat man said. "What evades me is why you are still here."

"I feel I have not done my best yesterday. I wish to try again."

"This isn't an audition, Spencer. You came, you failed."

The man tried to leave, but Chris put a strong arm against the gateway, barring him.

"I didn't think you heard me properly," Chris said with slow menace. "I think I am owed another try."

"Why should we let you?" the fat man replied with equal threat.

"Why not? If I suck again then I will go."

The man thought for a moment, then reluctantly nodded. "Go. See if you can impress. But be warned. You have a lot of ground to make up, Hunter."

The man pushed past Chris with unexpected strength and followed the others. Chris watched him leave, then headed back to his tent. Claire was already making breakfast, having quickly learnt how to use the solid fuel metal stove. Marty was still snoring. Chris went to tip him out of his hammock, but Claire's voice stopped him.

"He was late home," she said from the stove, not looking up from the steaming water.

"How late?" Chris asked Marty, who snored in response.

"Late enough." Claire stood beside Chris. "He's hurting inside, isn't he?"

"He is. I just wish I could help him."

A gentle hand led Chris away. Claire sat him down and lifted a small pouch from the water.

"You are. You've done more for him than anyone. You took a lost boy and made him an equal. Even in the smallest village a lost boy becomes property of whoever finds them. You didn't turn him into a slave. He's more like a brother."

"Or a son. He's been useful."

"He will be again. Let him find himself."

Chris watched the sleeping form in the hammock. "What if he doesn't want to come back when he does?"

"Then that's his choice. Let him make it himself."

"How the hell do you know so much?"

Claire smiled. "When you are forced to lie with men for money you have to learn to read them."

"Can you read me?"

"Yes, and don't worry. I understand." She stood and left.

"You could be in there," Marty muttered from his bed.

"You should be out here," Chris said, opening the breakfast pouch.

"Any for me?" asked Marty, rolling out of his hammock onto the hard dirt floor.

"In the pot."

Hugging his green sleeping bag Marty hopped like a fat grub until he sat beside Chris. He took the other pouch from the water, cursing at the steam that scalded his hand.

"When you've finished being dramatic we've got work to do," Chris said when Marty had stopped blowing on his hand.

"You're all heart, ain't you?"

"Known for it."

"Known for what," asked Claire, coming back in with a full water bucket.

"Not a lot," Marty replied, dodging a slap from Chris.

"Are you ok?" Claire asked Marty, seeing his red hand.

"It really hurts."

Claire went to take his hand, but Chris stepped in.

"Marty, we got work to do. Your hand's fine, so get dressed. We are back on the job."

Marty looked hurt, but hopped back to the car and dressed. Claire shot Chris a warning look, but broke into a smile when the old man winked back.

"What's the big deal then?" Marty asked. Chris was leaning on the flat bonnet of the Land Rover.

"We were kicked out of the competition, but they let us back in, on one condition."

"What's that?"

"We look good."

Marty smiled and pulled at his shirt. "Well, you know I always look good. Not much we can do about you though."

"Drop it, kiddo. This is serious. We gotta go in there and really make an effort."

"Such as?"

Chris dropped his shoulders. "I don't know. I thought the bang would have impressed, but they seemed to hate it."

"What about we just go in like Greg?" Marty asked, moving closer to Chris. Claire noticed when the true emotions came out, the playing stopped.

"I ain't dressing in furs and prancing around like a stupid dog on hot sand."

"I don't mean that. We got blades too. How about we make a more energetic show?"

"Like we would if they were real?"

"Exactly," Marty said, nodding. "Pretend they are sheep or something. We sneak up, make a fancy attack, then let them bang their sticks."

Chris smiled, making his face light up. "I think I know how to do it too." Marty looked puzzled, but followed Chris to the car. Claire watched with patient amusement as they took cloth from the back and tore it into strips. When they asked her to get some twigs from the nearby bushes she left without question.

Chapter 24

The Hunters stood in line, some missing from the day before. The stands were full of the best paying citizens and the announcer was calling the competitors forward one by one in a monotone voice. The official behind the screen kept pushing them onwards and sending the work teams out to herd the sheep into the arena, or clear the dead ones away. Already a large open coal stove was cooking the freshly butchered mutton.

"Spencer?" the official called.

"Ready," Chris said. He and Marty both carried a fat roll of some sort of cloth. They looked tatty and old.

"You have three sheep. Deal with them," the official said, ignoring the two men.

Chris nodded to Marty and they ducked down near the end of the screen.

The mayor sat in his official box with a tall thin man on one side, and a short fat man on the other. The fat man held a board on which the list of names was kept.

"Spencer is next, sire," the fat man said.

"Thought we agreed to remove him?"

"We did, sire. But he made a passionate plea, stating he would be more entertaining."

"Well," said the mayor, "he had better be."

The announcer called out Chris and Marty's names and the crowd waited for them to appear from behind the screen. And waited.

"This is poor form if they do not appear after their request," the mayor said.

The fat man was about to speak when one of the sheep gave a soft bleat and collapsed. The crowd watched as the knee length grass bent and moved as if blown by a gentle wind. It was a hot and still day. They held their sticks on their laps and watched. A second sheep gurgled a bleat and fell. The grass moved again, and suddenly stood up. The monster ran like a man, leaping into the air and drove it's dagger into the third sheep as it tried to run. Another creature rose, holding a small black blade of it's own. Pulling back their hoods Chris and Marty faced the crowd and bowed.

It took a moment for everyone to recover, but the sticks were soon pounding each other and there was even a cheer. The invisible men who moved like the wind made the ladies breathless and the men impressed. The announcer called on the next group, but they had to wait while Chris and Marty moved the dead sheep.

"Think that worked?" Marty asked, stripping off his Ghillie suit once they were outside the arena.

"What you reckon?" Chris replied, nodding to the arena where the sticks still clicked their approval.

"Good idea that, to hide in the grass dressed as grass."

"I'm just glad you took out that last one. I'm too old to be leaping about."

"I agree," Marty said, wiping his knife on his trousers.

The next morning the list was shorter, but Chris saw his name was now in the top five. Greg still kept the number one space.

Some of the other Hunters moaned when they found their names had been removed from the list, but slowly the tented village emptied.

"You impress me, old man," Greg said while Chris looked over the list.

"How so?"

"You are still here." Greg reclined on a bench near the beer cart. The barrels were being changed but Greg still had a wooden tankard of beer in his meaty hand.

"Does that impress, or concern you?"

"Impress. You cannot win against me. You have no show."

"No 'Flair'," Chris said, sitting near Greg.

"Precisely. You go into your work with the clean action of a butcher cutting meat."

"You've said this already."

"So I have, but still it remains true." Greg drained the beer and threw the tankard away. Ben caught it and pestered the carters to refill it.

"And yet you still persist in asking me to leave," Chris smiled. "I think you are scared."

"I never get scared," Greg boomed loud enough for everyone to hear.

"You do," Chris replied softly. "You are afraid that you will lose to someone who is a precision cutter. You'd lose to a butcher, not a Hunter."

"I know I cannot lose. What confuses me is why you stay."

"I'm here to see how everyone compares to me. See if I can learn anything from them."

Greg laughed so warmly that Chris felt himself try to join in. "You really don't get this life do you, old man. You have your fancy bang sticks. You are known for your skill. You work in a job that is always in demand, and you are reputed to be skilful and professional. These fools should be learning from you."

"Maybe I need to up my show then?" Chris said.

"It's not that." Greg shook his head and took the refilled beer from Ben. "There's some reason you are still here. I will find it."

Greg stood and strutted away, pointing to one of the pleasure women to follow. Chris watched the fur draped figure duck into his tent and leant on a table. He was old. He felt it in his bones. But he could still take down a target, and he could do it better than anyone. Greg was right. This wasn't his place, and Chris himself didn't know why he stayed. All he knew was that he was staying, and when he found out why, he could decide what to do then. Shaking the confusion away he headed back to his own tent.

"We still in?" Marty asked from his hammock.

"Yeah. Seems they liked it. We're up to the top five." Chris peeled off his camouflaged jacket and dropped into the collapsible chair. Claire took the coat and laid it on the side of the car.

"Top five eh?" Marty mused. "Sounds good." He turned away and pulled the sleeping bag over his head.

Chris shook his head with a smile and went to light the small stove. Claire stopped him with gentle hands and lit it herself. She then filled the rectangular metal bowl with water from the bucket and took the food pouches from the metal storage box in the back of the Land Rover.

"Thanks, but we can feed ourselves," Chris said.

"I know. I just want to help you." Claire slid the breakfast into the water and watched the yellow and blue flame as it licked the bottom of the bowl.

"You do that and we'll become dependent on you."

"I already am," said Marty's sleeping bag.

"I don't mind that," Claire said with warmth.

"I do," Chris said, trying to sound harsh. "You got your own life to live. You told your family you're free yet, or even alive?"

Claire shook her head. "It is a great shame for anyone to be sold into that kind of work. I would never find anyone to join with."

"So what will you do?"

"Come with you?"

Shaking his head Chris took a drink from the bucket. The sun was rising and the tent was warming up. The water was still cold from the night, refreshing.

"We can't take 'guests' in our work. We can drop you at another city. Best we can do."

"And what would I do in another city? Sell myself into another bed?"

"Sorry, but what we do is dangerous."

"So is my life," Claire said, standing to face Chris. "I have worked on the boats in storms, on the docks in winter, in the hot kitchens of the town hall. I have faced danger before."

"Our danger is one that eats you. You faced that?" Chris stared her down, seeing the crack in her resolve and wanting to hold her, to comfort her, but knowing he couldn't. "I'm sorry, but it's really too dangerous."

"You survive," Claire said, dropping back to the floor by the stove.

"And every day I wonder why."

"Me too," said the sleeping bag.

Chris slapped the bag, ignoring the dramatic moan of pain. "We live on the edge, in the wilds. Even the villages are unsafe. Raiders, monsters, wild animals, hell, even the ground itself tried to kill you. You get out there without water and you won't last three suns before you die."

"But if you don't take me away that's what will happen," Claire said with damp eyes.

"What you mean?"

"I have left the city, and not on official business. I could reapply to go back, but my family would refuse to support my claim. I would have no home. They don't let people in without family already inside. When you all leave and these tents are taken down I'll be left out here alone."

Chris cursed softly, then apologised. "Fine, we take you to a place we know you'll be safe. You may be bloody lonely for a while, but you'll be safe."

"Where's that?" Claire asked, tears slowly travelling down her pale cheeks.

"Where is that?" Marty asked.

"The bunker," Chris said.

"Whoa, wait a minute," Marty said, rolling out of his hammock. "You can't leave her there all summer. That's cruel."

"Why not? It's safe, secure, and she'll have everything she could ever need."

"What about your rule that nobody goes in there but us?"

"Piers went in there," Chris pointed out.

"Yeah, but that was Piers, he's one of us."

"So is Claire. She's an outcast, lost and alone, just like us."

Marty went to speak, the fire still inside, but those last words were like water, cooling him. Instead he grit his teeth and walked away.

"Is he alright?" Claire asked.

"Marty? He's fine. Weird but fine." Chris left the young man to walk it off, not too sure why he had become so worked up so fast. They had more Trials to face.

Chapter 25

They waited in line with the others for their turn in the arena.
Marty moaned that being popular meant they were on nearly
last and therefore had a longer wait. Chris just smiled in
anticipation. He was actually enjoying this, relighting some long
lost child deep inside. Today was going to be even better. They
weren't going to use the ghillie suits this time. Instead Marty
would use his newly grown muscles to wrestle a sheep down
while Chris silently took out the other three. This would be both
impressive and allow them to show their skills.

The time came and they went in. every day the number of
targets was increased, today from three sheep to four. Knowing
this Chris let Marty flex his bared arms and he moved with
stealth towards the nearest sheep. Chris melted into the grass.
While the crowd watched Marty pick up his sheep and throw it
they banged their sticks in appreciation. All the while Chris crept
towards the three that watched their companion in a weird
interspecies wrestling match. Marty held the wriggling sheep

down while he drew his blade. The sheep kicked out and the knife went cart wheeling away. Cursing Marty shrugged and pulled his pistol. He placed the scuffed barrel between the dull eyes and the sheep was stilled. The shot made the other three run towards nothing.

Chris grunted, but leapt up, knife in hand. He caught the first sheep as it ran past, slitting its throat as it pushed him. The second came on the other side and Chris threw the bloody knife from hand to hand, cutting the sheep down. The third turned and ran for the edge of the arena. Chris dropped the blade and drew his pistol. He followed the running sheep with the sights until it felt right, then he fired. The last sheep stumbled and rolled over. The sticks banged loudly from the crowd.

"Hunters Spencer and Fritz-Herbert," the announcer called as they were ushered away. The sheep were dragged away and the new ones let into the arena. Chris and Marty watched the next Hunter as he used a bow to attack the sheep. The silent arrows were effective, but inaccurate. The fourth sheep was wounded and ran for the edge. The sticks fell silent, showing the crowd were disappointed with the escaping target.

Greg was next. As usual he walked with confidence into the arena. He undid his pelisse and let it drop. Then he took his curved blades from his belt and half stooped across the arena. He kept low, letting the sheep see him and run. He herded them towards the centre, then threw his first blade. One sheep dropped, the other three splitting up. Greg threw the second blade and felled one of the pair. The other sheep ran back towards the centre. Greg left this one, moving over the large open area towards the single sheep. With his long blade he slashed at the dirty white wool, cutting the spine so the sheep fell. The sticks of the crowd banged louder and louder, nearly in rhythm.

Greg took a moment to pose, one leg raised onto the back of the dying sheep. He saw the other was making a run for the edge, the crowd falling silent as they watched. Greg looked unaffected, even pausing to adjust his hair. Then he lifted his long blade and reversed it. Holding the sword by the point, hilt above his head, Greg took his foot off the sheep and stepped back. Using his bulk he threw the sword. Everyone was silent as it spun lazily towards the last sheep. Greg was already going for his pelisse when the fourth sheep slid to a stop, it's black nose a foot from the edge of the arena. Greg retrieved his blades and wafted past Chris.

"That, old man, is how you do it," Greg said, leaving the thunderous roar of the sticks behind. Marty stuck his tongue out at Greg's back, but had to smile.

"He knows how to put on a show," Marty said.

"Yeah," Chris said, distant. He still looked at the fourth sheep while the officials removed it. "He can put on a show."

"We gonna be able to compete with that?" Marty asked. Chris just walked away.

Greg was the last Hunter of the day, so the others hung around the beer cart waiting for meat and beer. Greg sat in the middle with some hot mutton in a big bread roll. He talked incessantly to the other Hunters, daring them to try and contradict him. Chris ignored them all. Instead he stayed inside his tent. Claire had washed their clothes and refilled the water bucket. Marty considered cooking some food, but the sun was still too high for that. He exchanged glances with Claire as Chris brooded. Eventually Marty went out for drinks and food for everyone. He came back with a wooden tray on which was balanced three tankards of beer and three alcohol soaked bread rolls with hot mutton.

"What's wrong with you?" Marty asked Chris when he refused the meal.

"Nothing," came the defensive response.

"Seriously, you gotta eat. We did good today." Marty pushed the bread towards Chris.

"I ain't hungry."

"You're gonna be. Can't have a hungry Hunter."

Chris turned to Marty, frustration making his face hard. Marty braced for whatever might happen, but when the face broke he was lost. It looked like Chris was about to cry, but the sounds were laughter. As usual it was infectious and soon everyone was laughing with tears down their faces.

"What the hell we laughing about?" Marty asked. This made them laugh even more.

"I was thinking," Chris said when they had calmed down. "I don't think we can win this."

"That's not really funny much," Marty said.

"I know. What is funny is the thought of me being bothered. I admit this showy way of working is amusing, but not us. Why are we trying so hard to be liked?"

"To win?" Claire offered.

"Must be," agreed Chris. "Cos I don't do this normally. Usually I just turn up and do the job, no humour and no style"

"Damn straight," Marty said, making Claire giggle.

"Point is, why are we here, and what we doing?"

"You wanna quit?" Marty asked.

"Not really. Let's see how this goes. We got time to kill this season, and the work back home is getting slow."

"What about the people out there?" Claire pointed out.

"They need us, they know what to do. We get kids turning up every day asking for help. Out there they make do"

"We could be the only ones out there," Marty said.

"True, being worked to death or worse. There ain't much going on. This is like a holiday."

"What about the people you wanted to help?" Claire asked. Marty grimaced. This was a touchy area.

"They will live," Chris said, humour gone. He took his bread and left.

"I didn't want to upset him," Claire said.

"One thing you learn about 'im," Marty said, sitting beside her. "He only looks forwards, never back. The past don't exist, so don't be bringing it up."

Chapter 26

Jake struggled to stay awake. The same embellished tales, the same self absorbed monologue. Listening to Greg used to be exciting. Now it all blended into one. The man was still going, after five mutton rolls and more beer than Jake could count. Ben kept his usual neutral pose, waiting for instructions.

"We gonna be up all night?" Jake asked Ben, his voice lost under the booming tones from Greg.

"We stay until he goes," Ben hissed back.

"I'm hungry and tired. We were up all night polishing his blades."

"And we will be again tonight. Now shut up and wait."

"For what?"

Ben compressed his lips, holding his temper. "Until we are told to do something we stay by the boss," he said with low menace.

Jake shook his head and sneered, but stayed where he was. By biting his own lip he could stay awake. Greg was deep into another of his old stories, keeping the crowd in the palm of his hand. The officials watched from a distance, glad that the big fur clad Hunter kept the others under his control, making their jobs easier. A big hand waved an empty tankard and Jake jumped up, glad to be moving.

He went to the cart, feeling the chill of the night, the hot sun now a memory. Filling the tankard he saw one of the officials join him.

"Drink, sir?" Jake asked.

"Not on duty," the man said. "You're Jake Smith, right?"

Jake nodded. "I haven't done anything."

"I know. That's what confuses me."

"Sir?" jake asked.

"Why does he do all the work, and you just follow him around?"

"I help the best Hunter in the land," Jake said with pride.

"Do you? Interesting. Seems he does the work out there, and you are his joined woman."

"I serve him, not serve under him." Jake gripped the tankard in both hands and carried it back.

"Do you really?" Piers said to the man's back, too softly to hear. With a sly smile he went to see Chris.

Inside Marty was stroking Claire's face. They both looked shocked and embarrassed when Piers came in.

"Where's Chris?" Piers asked.

"Went walkies," Marty said, trying to move away from Claire without moving.

"Any idea where to?"

"Nope, sorry."

Piers nodded. "Thanks." He ducked out the tent, then back in. "And I didn't see anything." He winked, making Claire blush, then left. Walking the road that bisected the tented village Piers was officially checking everything was quiet. It was, with Greg acting to his audience. In truth Piers was trying to work out what Chris would do next. Not far, near the arena, Chris was doing the same.

That night the list for the next morning went up. Greg had talked everyone to bed, and now paced the deserted tables. His name was still top of the list, the position showing his popularity. His concern was that Chris' name was right below his.

"He is good," Ben admitted.

Greg glared at him, but stayed silent, brooding.

"He's not as good as you though," Jake tried. Greg cuffed Jake's ear and resumed pacing.

"What we doing about it then?" Ben asked.

"I don't know," Greg said. "This old man seems here to taunt me, to try me. I must not let him best me. But how to stop him?"

Jake opened his mouth to reply, but a glance from Ben showed it wasn't a question. Greg continued pacing.

"He had some style, and skill, that's true," Greg said, following his own personal monologue. "He is here for some reason I can't find. So can I use that? Maybe. What is he afraid of? What can I do that will bring him down?"

"We could hit his friend," Ben offered.

"Maybe. But that could only make him more determined."

"What about that woman he found?" Jake asked.

Greg froze, slowly turning. "What woman?"

"Story is she was sold to a pleasure seller, her family couldn't afford the debt. Chris took her away, paid the debt and she lives with him in his tent now."

"Perfect. If she wants to leave then he will take her."

"Why would he take some random woman and forfeit his place here?" Ben asked.

"He's that kind of man," Greg said. "He puts his own pride after helping others. He will leave if she tells him to."

"And if she won't tell him to?" Jake asked.

Greg smiled a nasty grin. "We make her tell him."

"That could work," said Ben. "But what if it doesn't?"

"We need a backup plan, something to make me shine over him."

"Killing something that threatens the crowds would do," Jake mused.

"Explain," Greg said.

"If something attacked the arena and you saved the people there, you would be a hero."

Greg beamed. "I like that. I will be the hero. I love it when I have such amazing ideas. I will find something big and scary to make them wet themselves, then stroll in and kill it. Then I will be certain to win. I'm so clever."

Jake rolled his eyes and even Ben looked annoyed.

"So how we gonna find this big scary thing?" Ben asked.

"You will," Greg replied. "Go out there and find me something massive. You have three days."

"How the hell do I find something big and scary, bring it back here, and have it attack at the right time?"

"I can't do everything, can I? You will find a way. After all these years with me you must have some of my amazing brains." Greg turned and strutted away.

"Good luck with that," Jake said to Ben.

"Hell, you're helping me."

"Can't. Gotta serve the boss." Jake ducked away and followed Greg. Ben sat on a table and looked to the stars for help.

Chris lay on his hammock and thought. It was quieter now nearly half the Hunters had left. The tented village seemed almost deserted. Thoughts flashed through his mind. Why was Marty so opposed to Claire living at the bunker? What would the next Trials be like? What would he do if he won? Why was he even trying? The biggest question was Greg. What was he going to do?

People like Greg didn't take failure easily. Their ego didn't accept they weren't the best. Chris had faced worse, and overcome them. Greg was just another challenge to face and defeat. But was it worth it?

Unable to sleep Chris rolled out of his hammock and walked outside. The sun was long gone but the heat stayed. A soft breeze helped, but it was still warm. Without a direction Chris wandered around. He nodded to the guards watching the tents, the man who came out to update the board, and another Hunter who was also taking a late night walk. In the clear air Chris tried to clear his mind.

"Give you something for your thoughts," Piers asked from a bench.

"You sure you wanna know?" Chris asked, sitting beside him.

"Sure. I'm in charge of safety here, and security. It's my job to make sure everyone is safe and secure."

"What the hell does that have to do with my thoughts?"

"Because, old friend, if you go nuts you have the firepower to kill everyone here." Piers smiled, but it was shallow.

"I'm not going crazy."

"Really? With you it's hard to tell."

Chris shoved Piers off the bench. "Thanks."

Smiling and rubbing his arm Piers waved away some guards who were coming over to help. "You know why you're here yet?"

"You are obsessed, you know?" Chris said. "I'm here. That's all that matters. If those flabby paper pushers in there don't like it they can come out here and say it to my face."

"Oh, but they do like you," Piers said. "You are second choice to win this."

"Really? Finally, someone appreciates us."

"They do. There is talk of how your guns can help them in the future. Some want you to win."

"Why?"

Piers winked. "Greg has style. He'd make a good puppet. But you, old friend, have technology. They can use that. Having you as their puppet would help them more."

"I'm nobody's puppet."

"Of course you are. You are a puppet to everyone. Someone has your strings and they control you. You follow the orders of your heart, your body, your work. I have plenty of people above me pulling strings too for me. None of us are free."

"But you choose who pulls the strings," Chris said softly.

"Yeah, pretty much. You wanna be careful. If you win it all you may actually use it all. Did you hear about Greg's sidekick?"

"No, which one?"

"Ben." Piers looked around, checking they were alone. "Story is he's off finding Greg some big finale, some fancy trophy to win the final trial."

"Figures. Thanks. You had any luck finding a home for Claire?"

Piers shook his head. "None. No respectful family will take the daughter of a disgraced man. It would damage their own credit."

"What about work? There must be something there for her."

"Nothing. Unless she goes back to what she did before nobody will take her on. I'm sorry."

Sighing, Chris stood. "So am I. For her I mean. she's not stupid, she has skills. Girl like that deserves a chance."

"You can take her with you."

"I could, but she'd be living in the bunker for the rest of her life. There's food, but that's no better than being in a detainment cell."

Piers nodded and shrugged his shoulders. "I agree. Maybe let her tag along until she finds a place she likes."

"Marty was doing that and he's still with me."

"Where is he?"

Chris was about to say Marty was back at the tent, but stopped. He saw the half smile on the security man's face, who nodded slowly when he saw Chris understood.

"He snuck back in just before I came over," Piers said.

"Makes sense. Maybe this is where he'll settle back down."

"Leaving a space on the car for Claire."

Chris shook his head and wandered back to his tent. Piers watched him, but didn't follow. Instead he went back into the city to keep an eye on Marty. The fishing boats would be out soon, ready to catch the early sunrise fish. Piers wanted to know which boat Marty went out on, just in case anything happened. Someone else had watched Marty leave, his fur pelisse rippling in the gentle breeze.

Chapter 27

The following morning Chris was up early. Marty was still gone, but the sun had risen and Chris didn't like to let the day pass him by. Even though he yawned nearly incessantly he still checked the weapons, equipment and the car with his usual compulsive care. Outside the other Hunters were either getting food or beer from the cart. Raised voices pulled Chris from the tent and into the road.

By the cart two Hunters stood toe to toe, red faced and screaming at each other. Chris looked for Piers and his security guards, but there were none. Knowing this could escalate Chris went to step in. fights between Hunters were becoming less frequent as the numbers dwindled, but they could still result in bloodshed.

One of the two men stepped back as Chris approached, hand going to a knife in his animal skin trousers. The other saw the move and raised his club, adjusting his grip with intent. Chris himself let his hand drop to his pistol, cursing inwardly when he realised it was still on the bonnet of the Land Rover. Instead he held out both hands.

"Be calm here, guys," he said with a soft voice. "We're all the same."

"He ain't," the one with the club spat. "He's a girly."

"I'm no girly, you old woman," the knife wielder replied.

"You're both a pair of old women," Chris said. "Now go back to your tents before security throws you both out."

"You call me what?" the club man said. The knife man also turned on Chris.

"I said you are both old women," Chris said. "Now go back to your tents."

"Or what?" the knife man said, slowly drawing the blade from his trousers and twirling the dull blade.

"Or security will make you go."

"Because you can't?" asked the club man.

"I can, I just choose not to."

Both men looked at each other, then attacked. Chris ignored the club that hit his left shoulder. Instead he focussed on the knife. He used his right arm to deflect the blade, ignoring the sliver of heat he felt when it caught his forearm. Using his now numb left arm he punched the knife man, then turned to the club man. Using his own hunting knife Chris was able to scare him away. The knife man recovered, but seeing the longer and sharper blade he backed away.

Looking at his dripping arm Chris went to sheath his own blade, but decided against it. Heading back to his tent he saw Greg watching. The big man had his arms folded, but he tapped his nose with one finger gently. Chris ignored the gesture. Inside his tent he found the first aid kit. Claire woke as Chris rummaged and insisted on washing and dressing the wound.

"It ain't bad," Chris said, pulling his shirt off.

"It is, but you've had worse I see," Claire said, noting the scars on his body.

"True. Just needs a wipe and a cover bandage."

"Can you go on?"

"With this? Of course. It's a cut, and a small one. I once had to fight with a broken leg, another time with no weapon at all. This is nothing."

"Looks bad," Claire said, pouring warm water over it.

"Stings like hell, but that's a good thing."

"Is it?"

"Yeah. Mean's it is clean and shallow. A deeper cut takes longer to register, and hurts a lot more."

"The voice of experience," Claire said sadly, taking a dressing from the black metal first aid box.

"Been there, stabbed that, got the scars."

"You shouldn't have let Marty leave you alone," said Claire while she wrapped the white bandage around his forearm.

"He's young, like you. Need to know when to put up the fence, and when to leave the gate open."

"But an open gate lets in others too."

"True, but I can take care of myself."

"What about your back?"

Chris cocked his head. "My back is fine, save a nice big bruise."

"I mean who is watching it?"

"Marty, as always."

"Is he?"

Chris was about to speak when Marty came in.

"What happened? I miss something?" he asked, looking at a shirtless Chris holding hands with Claire.

"Yeah," Claire said, standing. "You missed something, and Chris dealt with it for you." She pushed past Marty and left.

"What's with her?" Marty asked, noticing the white bandage when he walked around to face Chris.

"I think Greg wanted us out of the way so got a little fight organised."

"Really? What the hell. I'm gonna flatten that smug face of his."

"You will sit and be silent," Chris said. "He's scared, and desperate. He send that kid of his, Ben, to find something to help him win. Something impressive."

"How you know that?"

"Piers told me. We gotta be on the lookout for what he does next."

Marty nodded. "And if I get a chance can I level Greg?"

"When the time comes he's all yours."

Marty beamed and slapped Chris on the shoulder, who winced. Leaving Chris on the floor Marty went to get more water.

They lined up behind the screen, now only a few of them left. Greg stood at the back, with Chris in front of him.

"You seem to be doing well, considering," Greg said.

"Considering I'm not a fancy boy like you?" Chris shot back.

"Considering how old you are," Greg replied with a level voice. "Amazed you lived so long. Must be why the crowd love you."

"And you are here because of your amazing personality?"

"Naturally. That and my superior skill."

"Still waiting for that," Marty bridled.

Chris shot him a silencing look. "What you thinking?" he asked Greg.

"Oh, not much. How about for this last round we go back to basics?" Greg idly picked a fingernail with a short knife.

"Basics?"

"As in we use no fancy weapons, just our blades and our own strength."

Chris scrunched up his face as he thought, deepening the creases already there. "Sounds a plan. You gonna go in with just a knife too?"

"Of course. Let's give them a real show of strength."

Chris nodded and stepped forwards as the Hunter before him left to enter the arena.

"You are crazy," Marty hissed.

"Probably," Chris nodded, checking his equipment.

"You seriously gonna let him talk you into losing like that?"

"We ain't gonna lose, not like this."

"With no weapons is suicide. The sheep were bad enough." Marty rubbed his face with his hands. "The rabbits were annoying, and the cats were a bit upsetting to kill. But this is the last round. After this the last two go head to head. They ain't using anything cute and fluffy anymore."

"I know." Chris leant around the partition, watching the man before in the arena.

"So you know what we are up against?"

"I know. Look, we faced 'em before no worries."

"True, but that was in the open, and with guns. This hand to hand crap will only end up in us getting killed."

"We won't be killed," Chris said, patting Marty on the shoulder.

"How you so sure?"

"Like I said, we've done this before. We can do this."

The attendant waved them forwards. With a deep breath Chris walked around the panel. Marty shook his head but followed.

The stands were full as the watchers banged their sticks. The bloody mess was cleared and the other Hunter limped away. The ropes that made up the arena were now lined with boards to stop anything escaping. This wasn't about stalking anymore. This was killing. Blood was splashed on the beige wood in dark wine red stains. In the middle of the arena were four cages, the occupants slobbering and snapping at their handlers.

"We're going to die," Marty said in a sing song voice. Chris knew he was worried, but Marty was a Hunter and you never ran from your prey. If you did you become the prey and die tired.

"Just follow my lead," Chris said. They stepped into the arena and the handlers ran out, dragging the boards closed behind them. Four lengths of rope linked the cages with the handlers outside the arena. Chris walked the edge of the ring, looking over the boards. Marty followed, feeling a little lost.

Once he had done a full lap Chris looked over the cages, even poking a finger into one. The crowd gasped as the animal snapped at him, nearly keeping a finger for a treat. Chris smiled and waved his uninjured hand. The crowd banged their sticks again. Chris spoke briefly to Marty, sending the younger man to one side of the arena, then went to the other himself. With closed eyes they took a deep breath, held it, then opened their eyes and nodded. Chris raised a hand, held it, then dropped it. The handlers pulled on their ropes and the cage doors dropped open.

At first the wild dogs blinked at the open gate, then they ran. Moving as a single fluid blur of bodies they ran for the edge of the arena. Finding the boards blocking them they barked and howled. One noticed Chris and turned to face him. The others saw the bipedal intruder and as a pack they slowly stalked Chris.

The crowd watched with silent anticipation. Their sticks lay forgotten on their laps as Chris dropped his rifle and laid his pistol on the matted grass beside it. He watched the dogs as they drew close, the animals knowing their quarry was trapped just as they were, but the hunger inside drove them on. Chris walked backwards slowly with his arms held wide. Out of the corner of his eye he saw Greg watching, mouth wide in shock, but his eyes betrayed the amusement. He looked like he had won. Chris winked back, then gave a low whistle.

"Oi, fur balls!" Marty yelled from the top of the cage. Crouching like a hawk he drew his knife and flipped it so he held the blade between finger and thumb. He jerked his wrist and the blade appeared on the chest of one of the dogs. The others watched as it fell onto its side, then charged at the cage. Marty leapt off and ran for the board while Chris drew his own knife. Pausing briefly to pull Marty's from the dying dog Chris leapt onto the cages himself, feeling the ache of age in his knees as he landed. He whistled loudly, stopping the pack. They turned and snarled, foam dripping from starving jaws. They fanned out, watching Chris as Marty slid around the wooden barriers. Chris waited until they were close enough, then threw one of the knives. He tossed the other in the air and rolled off the cage. Marty collected his knife back when it landed and watched as the two remaining dogs chased Chris.

Letting out a whistle himself, Marty got the pair's attention and waited. Both he and Chris walked slowly towards the dogs, who kept turning to face the two men coming from opposite sides. Finally they broke apart, one going for Chris, the other for Marty. Chris let his dog come, and rolled away at the last moment. The crowd gasped as the dog leapt but only rubbed on Chris' shirt. Marty's dog went low, aiming for his legs, but hunger and panic robbed the dog of rational thought and Marty simply leapt over the running animal, letting his body weight drive the blade into it's back.

Chris rolled and held his arm, looking hurt. The dog had stopped, shaken its head, and turned. It saw Chris limping away and snarled. Lowering it's head it charged, keeping low. Chris kept his back to it, dragging one leg and holding his arm as he headed for the edge of the arena. When the dog was about to bite his leg Chris jumped, rolled and threw the knife. The blade hit the dog in the hindquarters, sending it tumbling into the boards. Walking normally Chris retrieved his rifle and pistol and bowed with Marty. The crowd roared, banging their sticks and even stamping their soft soled feet. As Chris and Marty were pulled away from the arena Chris smiled and winked at Greg. The fur clad Hunter shot him a look that would curdle milk that was still inside the goat.

"That went well," Chris said. They were walking back towards the beer cart.

"Well?" Marty asked. "That was nuts. Why'd we do it that way?"

"To prove a point, and to win some points too."

"Just because the furry freak says he can kill barehanded you go all stupid." Marty paused to fill a wooden tankard with beer.

"Not so, kiddo. Now the crowds love us for our flair, our ability. We are a sure fire winner here."

Marty rolled his eyes and drained the beer. "Yeah, whatever."

"You can't complain. You get tomorrow to relax. Final trials are the day after. You can go back into the city again."

"Yeah," Marty said without enthusiasm.

"What's wrong?" Chris asked. He stepped forwards and grabbed the younger man's shoulder when Marty tried to walk away.

"Nothing," came the irritated reply. Marty shrugged Chris off. "I just don't wanna go back in."

"Don't you wanna find your history?" Chris asked.

"I do, and I don't."

"What the hell does that mean?"

"Nothing." Marty turned and walked off. Chris left him to it, watching with concern.

Chapter 28

In the woods a long way from the city Ben stumbled into a riverbed. Luckily it was now just a wide, flat stream. He'd searched for what felt like a full season to find something for Greg, and so far nothing. He had cut himself on thorns, fallen from trees and now had a bruised ankle from sliding into this river. With annoyance he took a rock and launched it into the sluggish river.

"Find me something I can use he said," Ben spat to himself. "Something that will help me win he says. Come and find it your bloody self!"

Ben sat in the shade of a tree, listening to the river as it rolled downhill. The sounds soothed his temper and soon he felt relaxed. Filling his dry water pouch from the river he stood and tested his ankle. It hurt, but he could walk. Deciding to go back Ben climbed out the riverbank and back into the trees. It was only because he paused to look back at the river that he heard the sound.

Creeping through the trees he honed in on the noise of soft snorting and a strange infantile squeak. Behind a thick gorse bush he saw a nest. Three of the four eggs were broken, possibly before hatching given the dark stains in the dirt, and the signs of some animal trying to eat the remains. The fourth egg was also broken, but the flabby and uncoordinated baby was very much alive. About the size of a large turkey Ben knew he could carry it easily.

"Hello there," Ben said to the infant. "I think you would do very nicely for the boss, after a meal or two."

With a satisfied smile Ben took his fur lined shirt off and wrapped the infant in it. The baby tried to struggle, making walking difficult. But after a few minutes it gave in. Ben could see it could walk, so he'd have to carry it non stop back to the city. The prospect of a good full day's worth of walking didn't fill him with joy, but the knowledge Greg would love this thing kept him going. It had a lot of teeth, and with some prodding, it could make an excellent show stopper. Fighting this thing hand to hand would make Greg look like the true hero he was. Ben heard the sticks in his head as he walked. They were going to win.

Minister Rupert O'Keefe held his white robe around him as he walked out of the city gates. The guards let him pass, but they still looked with open suspicion. O'Keefe was used to prejudice from unbelievers, and gave his customary friendly wave. Heading alone past the beer cart he nodded with satisfaction that it now was deserted. With only two Hunters remaining there were no crowds to be here.

Walking down the dirt and stone road O'Keefe stopped outside Chris' tent. He heard soft sounds of sleep, and a gentle rustle of movement. With a loud cough he ducked inside. The square front of the Land Rover faced him. The utilitarian car fascinated the minister, who spent a moment or two looking over the strange contraption. He'd seen the convoy lorries many times, but this wasn't built to carry, it was built to fight.

"Can I help?" Chris asked, making O'Keefe jump.

"Yes, I certainly hope so, Hunter. I also hope to help you too."

"Ok. What brings you out into the savage wilderness?"

O'Keefe smiled and bowed slightly. Chris leant on the car, waving a hand back.

"You used to take the blood didn't you, once?" O'Keefe asked.

"I did. So what of it?"

"You know of the tale of the Samaritan?"

Chris sighed. "We heard it from a man who had one of the last of the Holy book. It was about someone who stopped to help a man, even though they were at war or something."

"Close enough. The truth behind that tale is much deeper of course. The Samaritan stopped to help a man who was dying. That made him ritually impure. He was unable to rejoin his family, to worship, or work, until he was cleansed, and that took days. So he helped someone he didn't know, and made his own life much harder, when others wouldn't help."

"And this has something to do with me because?"

O'Keefe smiled his friendly smile. "You are the Samaritan."

"I have no family, no worship, and not much in the way of status. Why would I be bothered by helping someone? Who did I help anyway?"

"Ms Shaw. She was needed to settle a debt of her family. You took her away from that debt."

"Claire? I paid that fat lump who cheated her, and probably paid him too much too."

"You did pay him back for the debt, but Ms Shaw hasn't been released. The businessman claims loss of earnings from your intervention. They cannot touch you of course, but I would suggest you and your associate stay out of the city."

"We ain't allowed in anyway," Chris said.

"That is true. But I think your friend does find a way in."

"I don't think he will now."

"Because of what I have just told you?"

"No," Chris shook his head. "Other reasons."

"That may be best. I hear tomorrow is the final Trial. I wish you luck, Hunter. They say the winner will receive riches, notoriety, and a permanent residence in the city. They already have the chambers for the Champion Hunter furnished and waiting."

Chris was about to speak when O'Keefe bowed and left. Chris stared at the tent flap for a while thinking. Something important had been said, and not just about Claire.

Chapter 29

Marty woke late having gone to the beer cart alone the night before. Inside he felt a whirlpool of emotions. The revelation he'd had the day before had shattered his entire life, his very belief in himself as to who and what he was. He wanted to talk to Chris more than anything, but he was terrified if the old man found out the truth he would tell Marty to leave, or worse still try to kill him. Marty lay in his hammock and pretended to sleep while Chris talked to the priest. It was clear what they were talking about, even though they tried to keep quiet.

Claire was snoring softly in her blanket nest. Marty felt something deeper for her, but he couldn't express it. Usually women were a temporary relief from the male condition known as arousal. They allowed him a brief respite from the urges he felt. He wanted to take Claire as his lover, maybe even as his joined partner, but he couldn't do it to her. His life was one of risk and danger. They'd had a lot of close calls in the past and he couldn't bear to see Claire weep for his death. Marty also felt that she would prefer Chris, naturally as he was her saviour from slavery. She owed him her freedom and had no way of repaying that except to join with him and serve him all her life.

She would have an easy life, that was true. Living in the bunker there was food and water for a small army. Shelter, clothes and heat it would be a perfect place to live in safety. But what if they were killed, or had an accident? Marty knew about memory loss. Now he knew about his past he wanted to forget it all again. If Chris and Marty were hurt then Claire would be left alone and forgotten, to live and die in solitude. That was worse than any kind of prison Marty could imagine.

Chris hung around outside after O'Keefe had left. He also felt caught up in the strong winds of change. He knew some cryptic message had been shared about himself and Marty, but he didn't know what it meant, what he should do about it. The final words of the white clad religious leader rolled around his head like beer barrels on a stone floor. A permanent resident of the city. The chambers are furnished and waiting. Why tell him that?

A soft hand touched his shoulder, making Chris jump.

"Sorry," Claire said. "I didn't mean to startle you."

"You didn't."

"Then why did you jump?"

Chris coughed to hide his reddening face. "That wasn't a jump. It was a Hunters reflex to a threat."

"You see me as a threat?" she asked with a flirty smile.

"Naturally. Anyone who sneaks up behind a Hunter is a threat."

"I must remember that. Or maybe I should shout boo instead?"

"Whatever," Chris said, laughing. "What's up?"

"Just wondering what you plan to do tomorrow."

Chris ducked back into the tent, shaking his head at Marty who was still in bed. "Win, really."

"Simple plan."

"The best kind," said Chris. "Most likely to succeed."

Claire nodded, looking slightly lost. She filled the square steel pan with water and lit the cube of fuel under it. Taking some of the now much reduced food pouches she dropped three in and sat by the cooker, watching the flames. Chris saw the light dance in her eyes.

"What you gonna do when we leave?" he asked her.

"I don't know," came the distant reply.

"You wanna go home?"

"I can't." She watched the fire but spoke from the heart. "If I return my family will be shamed. It's hard enough trying to make a living in the city without all this hanging over me."

"As far as I'm concerned since I paid the debt there was no history to be ashamed of." Chris sat cross legged on the floor, feeling the aches in his knees. While he spoke he stripped down his rifle.

"The debt is paid, but the shame remains. I could never find work now," she said.

"There must be something."

"There's work, but not any I care for. It's either being a tool of pleasure for men again, or working in the fuel factory. That's a nasty job. Not many live for long there."

"Fuel factory?" Chris asked.

"It's where the seeds are made into fuel for the convoy trucks. They do all these weird things to it and you get fuel. Some of the larger fishing boats have smaller engines that run off the fuel. They also make the maintain ace fluids to keep the engines running. Without that there's no supply."

"Don't you get your fuel in on convoys?"

"Sometimes, but mostly we get seed from the big city north of here. They grow it, we process it."

"What's the factory like inside?"

"I've never been." Claire watched the flames, her voice cracking.

"Is it that bad?"

"From what I've heard it is very good pay, but it has to be. The smells and heat kill anyone who works there for long enough. If someone works all their life they can provide for their family when they die, which won't be long."

"How long?" Chris sat opposite her, watching the light dance on her face in the soft darkness of the tent.

"Maybe thirty cycles if they are lucky. Oldest was about forty I think. It's slow, and nasty, but they all die."

"Do women work there too?"

"Only the ones who won't go and sell their bodies."

"So, you can't go back. What about going somewhere else?"

Claire looked up with red eyes. "Did you ever hear of a city letting in strangers from outside?"

"On convoy lorries yes. That's how they travel."

"But what about on foot?"

"No," Chris admitted. "Never on foot."

"Exactly. I'm exiled now. That means I can never go into a city."

Chris looked up at the sagging cloth ceiling, then back down to Claire. He had a smug grin on his face. "What if you just 'appeared' in a city?"

"Appeared?"

"As if by magic. You could say you rode a convoy and turned up there, looking for work."

"I would be asked about the truck I came in on."

"Ah, but you lost your papers. You were robbed as you walked around the city."

Claire pulled a face. "There is no crime in cities."

"There is, you just don't hear about it. Attractive young lady like yourself would be at risk walking alone near the convoy yards."

"So I was attacked, and lost my papers. Then what?"

"You ask the Law to help find them, which they won't. So you ask for work instead."

The damp and strained face watching him softened, breaking into laughter. The age she had gained this past few days dropped. She looked like a young girl again.

"That could work, if I could get in," she said.

"Leave that to me. I have my ways."

"You have a way to deal with anything."

"How I lived this long," Chris said.

"You could live quieter," Marty moaned. He rolled out of bed and drank some water from the bucket. "You think breakfast is cooked yet?"

Chris and Claire looked at the pot that was now boiling. Claire hissed as she pulled the pouches out. Marty looked at his then walked away. Chris waved Claire back when she went to stand, following the young man.

"What's your issue today?" Chris asked when he was out of Claire's hearing.

"Nothing," Marty replied, dismissive. He rummaged in the back of the Land Rover for a new shirt, throwing things around with more force than necessary.

"If something's wrong," Chris began.

"Nothing is wrong. Just leave me alone." Marty found a shirt and trousers and put them on.

"Can't. We live together, we work together, we fight together. Whatever is wrong we deal with it together."

"Not this." Marty went to leave but Chris grabbed his arm and swung him back around. For a moment he thought Marty would hit him.

"What the hell is up with you?" Chris asked.

"You mean what the hell am I?" Marty replied.

"You're Marty," Chris said.

"I am now. I wasn't always."

"You found your past?"

Marty bowed his head and nodded. "Yeah, and I wish I hadn't."

"Hey, it's ok. Whatever you did in the past doesn't make you anything else now."

"I does. It's me, the me I was before I lost my memory."

"Before the accident?"

Marty shook his head, still looking at the floor. Chris saw large raindrops fall near his boots, but the sky was clear.

"That wasn't an accident. Listen, I don't wanna talk about this right now. I just wanna go and think someplace away from here." Marty spoke slowly, his pain obvious.

Chris went into the inner tent, ignored Claire's questions, and rummaged under a stone in the corner of the tent. Walking back out he took Marty's hand and placed the small metal shape into it. The wet eyes looked from the hand to Chris.

"You serious?" Marty asked.

"Go. Sod off and find your answers, then come back and get me." Chris smiled and clapped Marty on the shoulder.

"What about the Trials?"

"I have some thinking to do about them myself, so the peace will do us both good. Just check your horizon in case your answer brings danger along."

Marty nodded and looked at the key. He hesitated, then threw his arms around Chris in a bear hug. He slid behind the driver's seat and waited for Chris to unhitch the trailer before he fired up the engine. With a weak smile Marty nodded then drove out, Chris holding the flap open for him. Chris watched the young man drive away down the convoy road and felt a weight lift, and another fall into it's place.

"Where's he going?" Claire asked, coming out in time to see the Land Rover climb the gentle hill leading away from town.

"He's found himself," Chris said. "Now he needs to find what to do with himself."

"Will he come back?"

"He'll be back, and more of a man than when he left."

Claire looked from the departing dust cloud to Chris. He seemed to be happy, even though his transport and his assistant had left. This new life was confusing, but she felt safe with Chris, and trusted him. Even in these uncertain moments she fell back on her trust. Still confused, but pushing the feeling away, she went back inside. Chris watched until the car had vanished into the heat haze, watching out.

Chapter 30

Greg also watched Marty leave, rubbing his hands and smiling.

"This will do very nicely," Greg said, mostly to himself. Jake watched and listened. "If he is alone now I have more chance to beat him."

"I thought you were going to beat him anyway?" Jake asked. He flinched when Greg turned to face him.

"I was always going to win. It's just now it'll be even easier. Could I ever lose?"

"No, not really," Jake said with a sigh.

"Of course not," Greg agreed, turning back to the fading dust cloud kicked up by the car. "I never lose, I'm too good to lose."

A whistle from their tent irritated Greg, but he went back to see who it was. Ben stood inside with a smug grin.

"I have what you wanted," he said.

Greg cocked his head. "Where?"

"Here." Ben stood aside to show the infant creature he'd found. It wobbled on shaking legs, but looked suitably dangerous.

"Is that what I think it is?" Greg asked, stepping forwards and holding out a hand to touch it. He was impressed when it snapped at him, missing his fingers by a blades thickness.

"I think so." Ben took a drink of water and kept his distance from the infant. "I found it abandoned in a nest south of here. It was half dead anyway but once I got it back here and gave it some meat and water it's looking a lot better."

"I'll say. Abandoned was it? Shame for it, good for us. Get it fighting mad, then hide it."

"Where?"

Greg laughed. "Put it in the tent next to Spencer. Knowing he sleeps with one of these monsters nest to him will help me sleep much better."

"What if he finds it?" Jake asked.

"He won't, because you will be there with it." Greg patted Ben on the shoulder and left, still laughing.

"Nice," Jake said.

"You asked for it," Ben said, poking the infant with a stick. It twisted it's head and nipped at the stick, biting it in half.

"How do we move it?"

"No idea. Maybe we wave some food in front of it and let it follow?"

"You fancy trying that?"

Ben shook his head. "Not really. Still, we have to move it somehow. Get some rope. We'll just have to tie it up."

Jake dropped his shoulders and left. Ben watched the infant with satisfaction. Greg always rewarded his favourite, and Ben was now easily in that category. That will mean less work, less effort, and more appreciation. Ben knew he was next to take over should Greg ever fall. for now he was willing to let the big man take the glory. His time will come.

Minister Rupert O'Keefe waved his aides away as he approached Chris' tent. He looked around quickly, then ducked inside. Claire was sat in the inner tent washing clothes.

"Can I help, Minister?" She asked.

"I was hoping to see Mr Spencer."

"He's out I'm afraid."

"So I see. Do you know when he will return?"

"I have no idea. He never tells anyone what he's planning, or even if he's going anywhere. I just keep myself busy and leave him to it."

"I noticed. You have kept yourself quite well here, haven't you, Ms Shaw?"

"What's that supposed to mean?"

"Nothing," O'Keefe said, smiling. "You have, as they used to say, landed on your feet. I know of your history."

"Good for you." Claire watched him warily, like a cat watches another cat in case it attacks.

"I know that you cannot return, and that Spencer had kindly sheltered you. My only concern is where you go from here."

"Why is that a concern for you?"

"The welfare of my flock is my concern. I wish to see only the best for you."

"If only that were true."

O'Keefe paused, chewing his upper lip thoughtfully. "I don't understand the reason for your hostility towards me, but I do understand where it stems from."

"I'm glad," Claire said flatly, without feeling.

"I also understand why someone helping an outcast would make you nervous." O'Keefe noted her reaction when he called her an outcast. "You must use this caution wisely."

"How? Listen to you and your Holy book?"

"Maybe," O'Keefe nodded. He turned and paced the edge of the tent. "There is something called gut instinct. For my faith that is the Spirit. For a Hunter it could be their professional experience. To a worker it may well be normal awareness. Everyone has that feeling when something is wrong, or right."

"So I should use your Spirit guide to lead me?" Claire dropped the clothes back into the bucket and watched O'Keefe with open hostility. "You think I should convert? Follow your faith? You think you can walk in here and lecture me of my evil ways and I will just agree and follow."

"I'm not trying to convert you, although naturally I would like it if you did. I am aware of a shortage of time, so I will be brief." The minister stopped pacing and faced her, his white robes swaying slightly.

"Be brief then."

"You cannot return to this city. That I am sure you are aware. However, my brethren are willing to shelter you in another city. You needn't take the vows or join our congregation, although, as I have said already, I would dearly love it if you did. They will find you shelter and work of your choice, within reason of course."

"Of course. And what will I be expected to do in return?"

"Nothing." O'Keefe smiled at her lost expression. "Ms Shaw, you know my faith and my calling. For us the act of helping others shows more of our faith than a thousand words. In helping you we may not be able to save your soul, but our actions will bring others into our faith. You will be a messenger for a cause that you yourself do not believe in, but through you the Spirit will do great works."

"Yeah, fine. So I just go with your brothers to another city and they will give me a job and feed me?"

"If it sounds unlikely I understand. When luck lands in your doorway it is usually followed by misfortune. In this, however, I can assure you there is no such outcome. We only want to further our faith, and through you we will achieve this. You find a home and a future, we find more souls to save. That is the price and you do not even need to pay it."

"Like your dead man you follow?" Claire looked sullen, like an unhappy teenager, but she listened.

"The Son is our role model, our guide. He gave himself as a sacrifice to show us how far we need to go to save the lost sheep. I hope you find your faith, but if you don't then faith will find others through you."

Chris came in, cutting O'Keefe off.

"Problems?" Chris asked.

"Not at all, Mr Spencer," the minister said, bowing slightly. "I was just checking Ms Shaw was doing well. I see she is. I came to see you as my main objective. May we speak outside?"

Chris nodded and they went back outside. In the glare of the evening sun O'Keefe wiped his short dark hair with a square of grey clothe from inside his robes.

"The attire is effective to lead, but a trifle warm in this weather," he said.

"Maybe you need a summer version," Chris offered.

"I will look into that." O'Keefe led the Hunter away from the tent, lowering his voice slightly. "I am concerned about the young lady. I have an offer to shelter her in another city. My brethren are willing to accept her as a stranger and find her work. She can have a future, a fresh start."

"Sounds good to me. You want us to take her?"

"That would be good. The convoys don't stop outside of the staging areas and trade posts so she could not get on one without entering the city. That is impossible here. If you could take her to a trade post we will provide funds and provisions for her to complete her journey."

"I will. We're nearly finished here anyway." Chris wiped his own forehead with his sleeve and looked at the sky.

"And a good thing too. Getting too damn hot here. Thank you, Mr Spencer. Knowing she is safe will be very comforting. I trust she will be safe with you and your assistant?"

"Marty? He won't touch her."

O'Keefe looked up and down the dirt road. "I noticed the young man left here earlier."

"He did. Said he needed to figure something out."

"I spoke with some of the fishermen in the city. He had lost his memory I believe?"

Chris nodded. "I found him with a bad gash to his head wandering lost. He knew his name, but not much else."

"Has he spoken to you about what he discovered in the city?"

"No. he seemed angry about something. He wanted space to think so I let him go."

"I see." O'Keefe chewed his lip again. "Then I will say no more. Thank you, Mr Spencer, for your assurance of the safety of Ms Shaw, and I hope you will take a blessing from the One on high?"

"I will, thank you."

O'Keefe held out a hand and laid it gently on Chris' damp brow. "May the Lord of all watch over you, give you wise counsel on all challenges you face, and keep you free from all the chains of slavery and sin." With a nod the minister left. He paused as he rejoined his aids, looking back. "Be free from the *chains* of sin and slavery, Hunter," he said, then walked away.

Chris considered following the tall minister to ask what he meant by chains, when Piers came out of the city gates, nodding to O'Keefe as he passed.

"You ok, boss?" Piers said.

"I ain't your boss," Chris said, watching the white robed man nod to the guards and vanish inside the city.

"You will always be. What's on your mind?"

"More than I care for. What's up with you?"

Piers cocked his head from side to side. "Not much more than normal. Just making my way in the world. I hear Marty's left."

"He had some issues to deal with, and the open road helps clear the mind."

"Is he going to be back in time for the final Trial tomorrow?"

Chris shrugged. "I hope so. But if he isn't then I will just go on without him. Better he isn't here, than he isn't all here."

"Fair enough. That minister, he's a strange one. You know he almost interrogated some of the fishing crews? Gave them a serious going over, verbally of course. Took some time but he got his answers."

"What answers?"

"To his questions. Mostly about Marty. Why I came out here. I wanted to speak to him, just in case. Will you have words when he comes back?"

"I will. This is getting a bit more mysterious than I generally like life to be."

"Yearning for the simplicity of the gun."

"Yeah," Chris agreed. "So, tomorrow is the end of it."

"Looks like. Hey, Piers? Is there really some residence for the winner?"

"Yeah. Big fancy place with grass and everything."

"Interesting." Chris looked at the high stone walls that bounced the heat from the sun onto the tents.

"Looks good to me," Piers said, following Chris' gaze. "And the winner gets to live there for the rest of their life, fed and happy. All they have to do is work for the city and compete in the next trials."

"They are having another Trial?"

Piers nodded. "Every four seasons. The winner has to compete against the others to keep their title."

Chris didn't answer, but he looked back to the gates. Chains of slavery and sin.

"So, let me know if Marty comes back," Piers said. "Make sure he doesn't go back into the city. There are some who want him, and not to have him over to eat with them."

"What did he find?" Chris asked.

"It's not my place to say. All I will say is the bond you two share, it is about to be tested. I can't say anymore when Marty isn't here to defend himself." Piers nodded and walked back to the gate.

"Why is everyone so bleeding cryptic around here?" Chris asked himself. He looked down the road, but he couldn't see the car. Marty would come back if he felt it right. Chris hoped he would. It was a long walk back to the bunker, and he had questions that were getting more concerning every minute.

Chapter 31

Greg watched from his tent. The silly religious fool had seen Spencer, then the city guard had spoken with him. Spencer was missing his partner, and the final Trials were tomorrow. With smug satisfaction Greg rubbed his big hands together and went back inside.

"He looks lost," Jake said, watching Chris through the flap in the tent.

"He's lost already," Greg said. "I know I'm too good for this Trial, and he never stood a chance anyway, but at least he was some enjoyable competition. Now he's out of it I won't be able to enjoy winning as much."

"Why not?" Jake asked.

"It is better to beat an opponent with skill, as a challenge, than easily winning against a lesser opponent. Those early trials were dull as the others' were weak. Spencer is good. Not as good as me, naturally, but good all the same. He made this a challenge.

Now his mind is away, and his partner is too, there is no challenge. Tomorrow I will win and he will lose."

"So you want our little gift still?" Ben asked, rubbing his arm where the infant had bitten him, a line of red marks from the teeth still showed.

"I aim to win tomorrow. That means no risks. We use the thing you found as it makes me look even better. I want those fools watching to remember tomorrow for the rest of their lives, and they will."

"Nobody will forget you," Ben said.

"It's hard to forget me, but time wipes minds, like Spencer's boy who has forgotten who he was."

"He's found out though," Jake said from the flap.

"Yes, that was most lucky for us," Greg agreed. He stood stripped to the waist, flexing his arms in front of a cracked mirror that they had kept on the cart. "I hadn't expected such luck, but then again, I'm too used to the world doing my will that I forget about it sometimes."

"And time wipes memories," Ben said.

"My point. Damn, I look awesome for tomorrow. Are my best furs ready?"

Ben nodded, holding out the pelisse. Greg turned it over in his hands. "Perfect." He threw it over his shoulder and looked at the mirror. "Perfect. I look every bit the winner. I hope we can choose our reward. I would much like a bigger glass to see myself."

"Maybe a powered cart like Spencer has?" Jake asked. Ben shot him a warning look.

"That is a good idea," Greg said. "I must remember that."

Jake winked at Ben and closed the tent flap. The two men stood behind their leader, waiting for his instructions. Tomorrow they would be victors and the big man needed to be ready, not for the Trial, but for the reception afterwards.

Chris was also thinking of his appearance tomorrow. Words and memories whirled around him like a storm. Ghosts of conversations mixed with things he'd seen, and could see coming in his future. Claire gave him a beer and began rubbing his shoulders.

"You don't need to do that," Chris said.

"I don't, but you do need it. You're like a gnarly old tree. I'll have no fingers left, but neither will you have knots."

"I'm fine." Chris wriggled to get away but Claire was good with her hands and soon he was relaxing.

"This is easier if you don't have the shirt," Claire whispered into his ear. Without thinking Chris unbuttoned his shirt and slid it off. The soft hands worked up and down his back, her breath on his neck. Chris closed his eyes and felt the world go soft, warm, friendly.

Claire massaged his back, feeling the scars and tension of a man who lives a life of danger. She felt something new, something imminent. The ending of something, and the loss of something else. Now more than ever she needed contact. She'd been promised to a man in the city, their joining was about to be planned when she was sold to the pleasure man. She had never laid with a man in a joined bed, and she knew somehow she should wait. But here and now with Chris, who was old enough almost to be her father, she felt a connection. He was handsome in a rough and worn way. Marty was more attractive outwardly, but Chris showed her compassion and that's what she needed more than looks and strength. Without realising her hands had moved around his body, stroking his chest. He seemed relaxed and so with a held breath she ran her hands down. The button of his trousers was stiff because of how he was sitting, but she managed. Only when her hand slipped inside the waistband did he react.

"What the hell?" he said, jumping to his feet.

"I just needed you," Claire replied, face down.

"Not like that. I'm grateful and all, but I'm too old for you."

"You treat me like an equal. No man ever has. I've either been something to desire, or something to perform a task. To you I'm me, a person free to do as she wishes."

"Maybe, but I'm am man free to not be doing things like that."

Chris finished his beer and stood. He looked at the sagging roof of the tent, the evening heat still soaking through. He went to leave, but stopped.

"Why?" he asked.

"Why what?"

"Why me? I'm not as attractive as Marty, and never tell him I said that."

Claire giggled, her reddened face cooling. "He's quite a sight, but I want more than something to look at. When I was old enough to be joined the man they chose was wealthy. My good looks helped me get the better choices of suitors. But he wasn't anything I would choose. That man you saved me from? Their choice of a man for me was even worse. He was a rich merchant, selling fish to the nearby villages. He went on about this rediscovered technology that could keep fish fresh for days, and how wealthy it would make him. I was just a trophy for him to show at dinners, and events."

"What happened?" Chris asked, sitting back down opposite her.

"When I was sold off he claimed he never knew me. Our joining was dissolved. I never saw him again. He didn't want soiled merchandise."

"And now you are free to choose who you want."

"Exactly," Claire said, looking into his eyes. "And I choose you. Out of all the men here you are the one I feel the most for. Tomorrow you face the final Trial, and then I guess you take me to another city and I find a new life."

"That's the plan, yes," Chris said.

"Then let me have this night. Marty is gone, most of the other tents are empty. It can be just you and me."

"I had someone once. She was killed and I swore I would never allow anyone to feel the hurt I did, or let myself be open to that pain either."

Claire placed a finger on his rough stubbly lips. "Hush now. This is one night. After the sun rises we will be two people again. Tonight let us be one."

Chris tried to pull back, but Claire leant forwards. Her plain cloth dress, opened at the back by her other hand while she touched his face, slid off her shoulders as she moved. She kissed him softly on the lips.

"Just for tonight," she breathed.

"Oh hell, I'm in trouble." Chris took her in his arms and kissed her back. Lying her down on the rough, hard ground she lay on her back and smiled as he looked at her body. He didn't look long before he ducked back down to kiss her.

Chapter 32

Marty drove until he was almost lost. He knew the way back, but he had no idea where he was. The instinct part of him waited until he found an open space, somewhere he could see just in case something was out there, waiting. He got out and leant on the wing, looking back at the setting sun. Inside he felt like a rock rolling down a long hill, smashing everything in his path. Something bad was in his history, and he didn't like it. How could someone who felt the way he does about life now have done what he had done?

His mind was still full of blank spaces, but some parts came back, like the images in a book. His parents on their ship, the money they earned, the people on their ship. The screams and tears and blood were memories he didn't want back. He had been a monster, worse than anything that walked the plains. It hurt to admit but he was worse than Parks, and that guy was insane. Could he live with his past now he knew it?

Walking around the car slowly Marty felt tears flow but let them. He knew he had to accept what he'd done, the crimes he'd committed. It would be hard, and he couldn't make up for the evil he'd performed, but he could do something about what he did from now on. Underneath his feeling of care and charity for other people could be his mind, the part that remembered, trying to repay for his actions. When Chris had found him Marty was dazed and lost. Chris had shown him kindness and helped a stranger, something nobody did these days. Could that be where his nice side came from?

Marty was terrified of himself now. He was that man once, and could be again. Like a monster that changes from man to beast and back he could return to his old ways. That was something he couldn't live with. But he had no idea how to stop it happening. Chris could help, but would his long time friend still speak with him once he knew the truth? They had been through so much, but this was something far worse, like finding your best friend is actually your worst enemy.

He sat on the flat bonnet and watched the sky ahead darken. Like his mind it lost the bright warmth of the day. The heat stayed, but the cloudless night went from dark blue, to almost purple, then black. As he sat Marty saw lights in the sky, like he saw every night. No matter how dark the night was, those lights were always up there. They guided the lost, helped illuminate their way. In darkness there was always light, if you looked hard enough for it. Even the darkness inside him had light, and light was more obvious than dark, and more useful.

Chris once said that there was a darkness in all of us. It fought with the light side constantly. Every nasty thought or act was competing against kind acts and nice thoughts. He was a battlefield now for light and dark, and it was one he couldn't win by himself. Once the final Trial was over Marty decided to tell Chris all and let the old man decide what to do. If he was willing then Marty would accept his help. If Chris couldn't forgive then Marty would understand and go his own way.

With his mind made up Marty got back in the car and turned around. Using the dim glimmer of the set sun he felt like a load was lifted from his shoulders. He was heading back to the light, both in mind and body. Chris would help him to deal with his past, he'd have to. If they carried on together someone would recognise Marty and know what he did. It was a miracle nobody had so far. Feeling happier and relieved, Marty drove back to the city. He had a future to build.

The sun was lazily rising when Greg met Chris by the beer cart. With only two of them left the cart was empty now, the organisers not considering two men and their staff to be worth the effort of refilling the barrels. They faced each other over a table, Ben and Jake standing behind Greg.

"I see you are alone, old man," Greg said. "Did he run away?"

"No, he didn't."

"Then where is he?"

Chris smiled. "He'll be here. I can win by myself, and I will win. I promise that."

"You really believe that?" Greg laughed loudly. "You have no idea old man. You had lost before this even began. I have style, skill and flair. It's my name after all."

"Only because you gave it to yourself," Chris said. "I hope you're ready for the final Trial. It will be quite the surprise."

"Not as big for me as it will be for you. See you in the arena."

Greg went to leave, but the sound of an engine stopped him. The Land Rover slid to a stop behind Chris.

"You ain't winning this," Marty said, getting out and taking his rifle from the holder. "We are."

"You are back together. That's nice. The family that loses together should stay together." Greg laughed again and left.

"We'll show you in the arena. You'll see we are the best," Marty called after him. Greg waved a hand in the air as he walked back to his tent.

"So. You came back," Chris said.

"Yeah. I need to talk to you, but after this. It can wait, and I can too."

"Fine. But we need to talk now about this, and it cannot wait." Chris took the keys from Marty and drove the car back into the tent. Claire watched with shining eyes as Marty came in. The young man kissed her hand, then went to look over his kit.

"What you need to say then?" Marty asked.

"It's about Claire, and the Trials," Chris replied.

"What about them?"

Chris took a breath, saved from speaking by Claire when she hooked an arm around his waist.

"Oh. I see." Marty coughed, embarrassed. "If you guys need the space I can go."

"I need you today for the Trial," Chris said.

"I mean after today. You go your way, I go mine."

The smile that grew on Chris' face irritated Marty, until he realised it wasn't there because he offered to leave.

"You will always ride with me," Chris said, moving away from Claire. "We are family, of sorts. We stick together no matter what."

"Yeah? Well you may want to rethink that after I tell you what I need to. But that can wait until tomorrow."

"Until tomorrow," Chris agreed. "We doing this final Trial first?"

"Sounds a plan. What are we doing anyway?"

Chris led Marty to the arena. To one side were more cages of dogs. The boards around the ring were stronger and there was some strange netting above so the people in the stands could see through, but were safer.

"I think we get a full pack," Chris said, waving to the cages.

"Can we take on a full pack without guns?"

"Possibly, but I don't fancy losing a leg just to gain favour. I think we do it our way. We've been playing up to the crowds too much. Time they see real Hunters working as they should. The professionals."

"That's not very fancy," Marty said, looking into the cages. "They like style and flair."

"They also like to see people being ripped apart by dogs. I'm not doing that. We go in, we do the job, we leave. Just like always."

"And if we don't win the Trial because we're too plain?"

Chris smiled. "Then we shouldn't win."

Marty frowned, then smiled back. "Maybe so. Been here far too long anyway. Time to go back to our own ground."

"Exactly. We will drop Claire off at a trade post on the way back to the bunker." Chris started walking back to the tents but Marty stopped him.

"Drop her off? I thought we were taking her with us."

"Where will she live, sleep, eat? Seriously, Marty. This is no life for her. If something happens to us she will live alone and that is not right. Best she goes to a city and starts a new life."

"But no city will take an outcast, you know that."

"O'Keefe has sorted it. We drop her at the nearest trade post and they have arranged transport on a convoy to another city. There she can start again with a new name and a new life. They'll even find her work."

"Sounds too good to be true."

"It is," Chris admitted. "There's a catch, but luckily for us and Claire we don't have to do anything. They hope the kindness they show her will help their movement."

"Movement?"

"Their religion. I understand it. I used to follow them. Now, it's just luck and faith we have to rely on. That and our weapons so let's go check them."

Chris put an arm around Marty's shoulders and led him back to the tent. Greg watched from a distance.

They walked into the arena as a group. Greg kept to one side as Chris and Marty walked in. the crowds banged their sticks, making the caged dogs bark louder. The announcer held up a hand for silence, the crowd slowly obeying.

"Today, honoured guests," the announcer said through a speaking trumpet, "we have the final Trial. These men before you are the best of their profession. Today they battle to claim the title and post of champion. Today you get to see who is best. The Trial is the hardest test of all. In the centre are fifteen wild dogs, captured from a pack that used to roam nearby. Three men died and one lost a leg capturing these dogs. Each Hunter will face them, fifteen per Hunter. The one who proves the most successful at their extermination will be selected as champion. Good luck, gentlemen. You will need it."

Greg stepped forwards, flexing his huge arms. "I do not need luck. Please gift mine to my opponents. "The crown murmured admiration. "I have the strength of body and speed of mind to deal with this threat over the wisdom of age, and the endurance of youth my fellow Hunters have. This I will prove before you, but I allow them the first attempt." He bowed and winked at Chris. "My grand finale."

Chris rolled his eyes as Greg bowed to the crowd and left, followed by a wave of banging sticks. Marty had his old happy grin back, and that calmed Chris. With all the problems the young man had been going through for this they needed to be fully focused on the job.

"You gonna be ok with this?" Chris asked, half turning from the crowd.

"You really need to ask?"

Chris laughed. "Not really. One last time then we can go home."

"Then let's do this then."

They shook hands and moved to opposite edges of the arena. Chris waved to the announcer, who held up a hand to quiet the crowds.

"Firstly on behalf of myself and my partner," Chris said loudly, "I would like to thank you all for coming out, the organisers for laying all this out, and those Hunters who competed with us. This has been a show of prowess and skill. Now we would like to show you true Hunter skills. This is how we deal with these threats in the wild outside the cities. Enjoy."

The sticks banged again as the handlers hooked up the ropes to the cages. Moving behind the board and net boundary of the arena they watched Chris, who nodded to Marty. A solid click of a cocked rifle told Chris all he needed to know. With a low whistle he loaded is own rifle then waved to the handlers. The ropes went taut and the dogs were released.

Marty leapt onto the cages, this time spaced only two high. This meant the dogs could jump onto the cages and get to him. They circled Marty on the ground, watching him with hungry eyes. Chris knelt and aimed. His rifle spat rounds into the dogs, putting fingernail sized bullets into their heads. One by one they dropped until after fifteen rounds were fired all fifteen dogs lay still. The crowd were silent, trying to work out what they had just seen. It was over in a moment.

Chris shouldered his rifle while Marty checked the dead dogs.

"That is how we do it in real life," Chris said. "Nothing fancy, no flair. Just in and out. If that's not entertaining enough I apologise, but when your life is on the line you do the job as quickly and cleanly as possible. A carpenter may take days on a piece of timber, but he won't do it to amuse anyone watching. He does it cleanly and quickly to achieve the results required. This is what we do, and this is how it is done. Thank you for watching."

He led Marty out past the still silent crowd. Greg watched from the sides with open joy.

"You think they didn't like that?" Marty asked when they were out of the arena.

"I don't really care too much. We do the job our way. Those were no ordinary dogs. They had been starved and beaten. They were savage. If old Greg survives then he is better than us at doing it the hard way and deserves to win."

Marty shook his head, but inside he agreed. This wasn't a competition for ability or skill. It was for entertainment, and that was something they didn't excel at.

Chapter 33

Claire heard the sounds of shots fired, counting them. She knew the test, and when the fifteenth shot echoed off the city walls she knew they were finished. Soon they would be back and she would be leaving with them. Inside she missed her home, her *old* home. She missed her family and friends, and was upset she could never see them again. But she also knew she could never go back so she had to go forwards instead.

Looking over the old Land Rover she thought of the adventures it had been through. It certainly looked menacing, like a wild dog that was only sleeping, waiting to be woken and fight. She walked near it, but didn't touch it, just in case. All the clothes and equipment had been packed away so she had nothing to do but wait. Chris had told her to wait in the tent so she waited.

The strange sound came from the tent next to them. It had been quiet overnight, just a heavy breathing and wheezing sound. Now it made a noise like a tiller on a boat that needed greasing. The low and long groan was unsettling, but the deep thud was terrifying. Claire shrank back to the car, feeling the cold metal in the heat of the tent. Her skin felt damp as she fought back the trembles that made her legs wobble. Another thud, like someone dropping a heavy roll of sail cloth, then another. The tent became dark as something massive blocked the sun.

Her heart pounded in her chest as she panted in fear. She wished Chris was here. He would know what to do. She could run and find him, but whatever it was had her frozen in fear. Outside men were shouting, unfamiliar voices. The shadow moved and the tent began slowly to bow inwards. The wooden pegs slid from the baked solid ground and a dark green and grey nose, like a frogs, slowly moved into the tent. She wanted to scream, to run, but she was frozen to the ground.

Another shadow darkened the first and the head stopped moving. It was so big it moved her tent even though it was trying to get into the next one. She wanted to scream, but her throat was as dry as the soil beneath her feet. The men outside were quieter as they moved away. Then the head stopped, it was now almost nodding slowly. The groan from the next tent stopped and turned into an excited squeak. The first head lifted, taking both tents with it. When Claire saw what the head was attached to her voice opened and she screamed.

Chris heard the sound before Marty, but they both broke into a run together. The arena was away from the tents, hidden by a thin stand of trees so the people watching only saw the ring before them. As they ran through the trees Chris saw a tent rise up in the air. The familiar body below the tent told him all he needed to know. He grabbed Marty and pulled him down beside the last tree.

"What the hell?" Marty asked the tree.

"I've never seen one go this close to a city before, save that one Parks made a hole in the wall."

"Make that two." Marty held up a hand and the tented Allo was joined by another. The screaming had stopped.

Men from the city ran out the gate, saw the creatures, and ran back inside. The first Allo managed to remove the canvas, using it's back leg to hook it off. The other had something in it's mouth as they walked towards the trees. Both men hid behind the tree as the bodies loped past. Chris couldn't see what they carried, but he knew it wasn't Claire. Once the thick tails were in the trees they ran to the remains of the tent.

The Land Rover lay on it's side, the trailer behind was nearly flat where one large foot had stepped on it. Their equipment was scattered everywhere. Marty checked the car while Chris searched the collapsed tent.

"Found her?" Marty asked from the car.

"Not yet." Chris pulled at the canvas until his arms ached. Sweat poured from his face as he tried to move the mass of cloth. Marty joined him and finally they cleared the inner tent. There lay Claire, half buried. She looked ok.

"Hi," she said weakly. Any hopes she was unhurt were lost when she coughed, a thin line of blood running from her mouth.

"You ok?" Chris asked, feeling stupid for asking such a pointless question.

"Been better." Claire coughed again, spitting more blood onto the ground beside her head. "Think I may have a problem."

"You'll be fine," Chris said.

Marty lifted the canvas that covered the rest of her body, then shook his head. Chris saw the mess of bone and blood. He fought back tears as she smiled at him.

"It's ok," she breathed. "You did all you could."

"I should have done more."

"You saved me. You promised I'd be a free woman, and I am. Thank you."

Chris held her hand, feeling her strength fade. Those shining eyes dulled.

"Claire?" he asked, voice a hoarse whisper.

"Still here," came the soft reply. "I'll always be with you. I'm free, and you are free too."

"What about me?" Marty asked.

Claire closed her eyes but still smiled. "You're not free yet. But you will be soon. Then you can be free together."

"I'll never forget you," Chris said, tears flowing openly.

"I know." Claire opened her mouth to speak, but her final breath was all they heard.

Piers came running into the remains of the tent, nearly crashing into the Land Rover.

"What the hell happened?" he asked. "What's going on?" He saw Claire and fell silent.

Chris stayed by her side while Marty motioned Piers to help him right the car. Once it was back on four wheels they leant on the side of it and watched Chris. In the midday silence the heat was heavy, but not as heavy as the feeling of loss.

Screams from both genders but equally urgent pulled them from their grief. The sound that froze the heart no matter how hot it was rolled around the hills. Marty knew it, Piers did not, but both knew it was trouble. Marty took a rocket tube from the car and waved to Piers to follow. Chris laid Claire's hand on her chest and stood. Ignoring both men he took a rocket tube and walked back towards the arena. Marty shrugged and followed. Piers hesitated but took a rifle from the car and ran to catch up with Marty.

Chapter 34

Greg finished his display and removed the dogs with his usual style. The crowd loved it and when it was over they banged their sticks loudly, some even breaking them. Greg stood on a pile of carcasses with his big arms up in the air, looking the mighty Hunter. Ben and Jake watched from the edge, but left Greg to take all the attention. Jake heard the scream from the tents, but Ben told him to stay put. Greg had planned to use the infant when the final decision was made and both he and Chris were standing before the crowds ready to be given their verdict. If Chris won the infant would be released and Greg would defeat it, winning himself the prize. If he had won anyway the infant would be killed and the body dumped in the woods. Either way he knew he had won.

The sticks banged in a wall of noise, like a field of crickets. Greg basked in the glow of their adoration, slowly noticing the sound die down. The people in the stands were no longer cheering him.

They were silent, almost in shock. Greg turned to see why, then stared.

Just outside the arena two adult Allosaurus stood watching. One had the infant in it's mouth, not dead, just being carried. It slowly lay the animal down and it stood on wobbly legs beside it's parent. The other Allo watched the crowds, slowly moving it's head from side to side. Waiting.

The crowd was silent, frozen in fear. As the more wealthy of the city residents they were used to luxury. Danger was distant, something that happened to other people. They had heard of these giant monsters from tales and stories. Now faced with them they paused, unsure what to do. Finally, one woman's body decided for her. She opened her mouth and screamed. The Allo snapped its head towards her, lowered its body down and roared. The crowd broke, flowing like a river of limbs and heads as they ran for the city.

Ben and Jake looked to Greg, but their leader was frozen on his pile of dogs, arms still held out. The adult dinos walked past them all, spreading out so they almost herded the running people. The infant ran after them, struggling to keep it's balance. It stopped when it saw Ben, roaring in a weedy squeak. Jake took one of Greg's spare blades and faced the infant. Ben saw a chance to stand out and took the blade from Jake. As Ben moved towards the infant Jake started walking away. Ben was about to shout at Jake to come back when the shadow fell over him. The infant squealed it's tiny roar and Ben dropped the blade and ran. He managed three steps before the head came down and all went black.

Greg was stuck. His mind and body were in conflict. The part of him that lived on success, on praise, was the first to run. Instead his primal instincts took over. He froze, staying perfectly still, arms still raised to the empty stands. He head Ben scream, knew it was him from his voice. Screams mixed with shouts of terror. This was all his fault. He had told Ben to take the infant, had caused all this. Now he had to deal with it. As the realisation dawned his body came back under control. Slowly he lowered his arms and took the long blade from his waist. He'd faced one of these before, and that was in their territory. This was his and he knew how to kill them.

Running from his pyre of dogs Greg sprinted towards the first Allo. Screaming a war cry he charged. The Allo looked back, jaws bloody, and stopped. The crowd that it was chasing also stopped, waiting. They were like lost sheep, Greg realised. They needed to be shepherded.

The Allo lowered its head to a few feet above the ground and roared. Greg roared in return. He dodged the head as the jaws snapped shut, sliding underneath. Fire flared on his thighs as stones and dirt shaved his skin but he ignored it. On his feet and still running he used the sword blade to slice the inside of the Allosaurus' legs. It roared in anger and pain, turning back to face him. Greg stayed underneath, keeping away from the head, staying between the massive legs. He kept slashing and stabbing, feeling the fire of adrenaline in his body. Either he would walk away, or the dino would. Only one would survive.

Waving the sword blade Greg screamed, his voice mixing with the dino's cries. Then one leg moved sideways, kicking Greg hard. He flew out from under the body, spinning in the air. When he landed it was hard on his back. The sword flashed in the sun, landing blade first in a tree, swaying slightly. The Allo looked at Greg, slowly walking forwards. Blood poured from it's wounds, but it still strode with purpose, as if nothing was wrong. Greg watched through the blur of his confused vision, head ringing when he had hit the ground. He saw his attack had done nothing.

Jake ran from the side, charging the Allo. He held a blade in each hand, both as long as his forearms. He leapt and drove them both into the monster's side. The Allo roared and turned.

Jake held onto the blades, fixed to the massive ribcage. The Allo bit at Jake, but he was too close to the neck, out of reach of the jaws. The neck was too thick for the head to reach him. Greg saw the stalemate, knowing it wouldn't last long. He tried to stand, but the world turned like he was drunk. He staggered and fell. Jake screamed as his grip failed on the bloody knives and he fell onto his back. The Allo stood over Jake, jaws waiting.

What happened next Greg could never recall properly. His vision still swirled, but there was a flash, and the head of the Allo burst like a rotten fruit. Blood went everywhere. Then some rapid bangs, like thunder but shorter and sharper. He blinked and shook his aching head, trying to clear his eyes. He could see Jake was still on the ground, but unhurt. The Allo lay on its side, the head missing.

Chris dropped the rocket tube and took his rifle, pumping a full magazine into the dying dino's body. Reloading he went after the next one. He saw Jake on the floor, the skinny man holding his arms up for help. Chris ignored him, letting someone else deal with the kid. With a habitual check of his weapon Chris pushed past the crowd that watched him and followed the screams. The rest of the spectators had moved towards the city, and were now trapped against the walls that used to protect them. The city guards refused to open the gates in case the Allo followed them in.

The final dino watched the trapped crowds, knowing they couldn't move. To their left were the city gates, to their right a bulge in the wall, in front was death. Most faced their fate with reluctant acceptance. Some cried and a few went to their knees, hands clasped together. The Allo watched, turning it's head to one side, swaying slowly to see them with both eyes. It roared, silencing the cries and prayers.

The Allo suddenly looked puzzled, turning away from the people. Chris stood alone, rifle in one hand. His knife lay hilt deep in the Allo's tail. It looked Chris up and down.

"You murdering bastard," Chris said, tears cracking his voice. "You prehistoric evil murdering bastard." He clenched his teeth and pulled the trigger. Thirty rounds chased each other into the massive head. The Allo roared in pain and shock, shaking it's skull to clear the hurt it felt. It looked back at Chris but he had already reloaded, sending another magazine after the first. When the Allo roared, mouth wide open, at Chris he stopped firing and gripped the magazine. There was another trigger and the grenade launcher coughed as the fist sized projectile went down the throat. The muffled bang, and the almost comical smoke from the dino's nose, preceded the slow collapse of the creature. Chris walked over to the fallen dino, the eyes glazed and unseeing. He aimed the rifle and fired into the eye until the rifle clicked, empty.

Marty came over with Piers. They stood behind Chris, not disturbing him. He still held the rifle to the eye. The crowd watched, waiting. With a deep sigh Chris lowered his rifle and walked away. He passed Piers, who nodded, and paused by Marty.

"Let's go home," Chris said. Marty nodded and they walked back to the car.

Chapter 35

Both Chris and Marty helped clear up after the attack. Amazingly only four people had been hurt, none of them badly. Chris reckoned it was the amount of people that confused the Allo's, delaying them while they chose who to attack. The stands and arena were damaged, but only Ben was killed, and Claire.

Chris carried her body wrapped in grey rags to the grave he had dug for her. Jake leant on his spade, digging another beside it for Ben. Marty walked behind Chris, head down. Piers followed, leading a small group of the city's residents. O'Keefe waited by the grave. He nodded to Chris, who laid Claire down gently beside the hole in the hard earth. It was only just big enough he noted with sorrow.

"People," O'Keefe said, addressing the crowd. "Today is a day of pain, but also of peace. Two of our following were taken, but they are at rest now, where no pain or sadness can find them. While we live in the harsh and unrelenting world, they are in the luxury of the eternal realm. Their bodies may have succumbed to time and eventually death, but their souls will never die, never suffer, and they wait for us when we join them. Now we lay Claire Shaw's body to be reclaimed from the clay we were formed from, for the divine potter to remould into another earthly vessel."

The minister stepped back and Marty helped Chris roll Claire's body into the hole, wincing slightly at the dull thud it made when it hit the bottom. Jake watched, then took a large sack, patted it gently, then lowered it into his own hole. It was all he could find of Ben, but it was enough for him.

"We rise, and we fall," O'Keefe continued, "as countless men have risen and fallen before us. And we look to follow them to the eternal realm of the Creator." The minister took a hand full of dirt from each hole and sprinkled it over the bodies. "Time to grieve, and time to heal. Time to recover, and time to react. Time to rest, and time to move on."

With an elaborate hand gesture O'Keefe stepped around the grave, pausing to lay a gentle hand on both Jake's and Chris' shoulders. His lips moved silently, then he left. The crowd walked around the graves, looping back around towards the city. Most looked to the trees in the distance, just in case.

"He was an ass," Jake said when the crowds had left. "He always said he was going to be the next Hunter, if Greg left or was killed. I never doubted he would be."

"He was a special guy," Marty said.

"How do you know?" Jake asked with sudden rage. "You never spoke to him. Either of you. You just laughed and waved your stupid bang sticks around." Turning on his toes Jake stormed back to the tents. Marty went to go after him but a low and familiar whistle stopped him.

"Let him be," Chris said.

"Yeah, I guess you're right." Marty squatted down by the hole and took some of the dirt. He stood and held it out to Chris, who took it with a damp eyed smile.

"A time to rest, and a time to move on," Chris said, sprinkling the soil on the grave. "That is what we will do. We need to rest, and be ready for the trip home."

"You want me to stay?" Marty asked.

"If you want. You knew her too."

"Not as well as you did."

Chris snorted a soft laugh. "True, but not as well as you may think. She wanted her new life, but had to leave her old one. That's why I lay with her. That's why I miss her, why I grieve for her, but no more than I would for anyone else."

"You are a terrible liar," Marty said.

"I am, aren't I? You know, I only ever loved one woman before her, and she was my wife."

"So everyone you love is eaten or murdered?"

"So it seems."

Marty stepped back. "I hope you don't love me."

"You? Not really. You annoy me."

"Good. I'm glad to hear it. You'll let me know if that changes?" Marty tried to make light of it, but he saw Chris wavering. He wrapped his arms around the old man and felt him collapse into sobs of loss.

"Damn it, but why her?" Chris asked through Marty's shirt. "She had so much to live for."

"I don't know, but I don't think we are supposed to know. We just do what we are made to do, and that doesn't involve understanding things like this."

"What the hell was I thinking going out and leaving her alone?"

"You couldn't know."

Chris gripped Marty's sides so hard it hurt. "I should have had her watch the show, been with me where I could keep an eye on her. I should never have left her alone."

Marty pulled Chris off and tapped his face. "Listen to me. I know it hurts right now, but you did nothing wrong. Yes, so she's lost her life of freedom, but you gave her that life to live. Without you she'd be in that city now being raped by whoever could pay the most coin. You saved her, and even after all this she's still thankful to you. So stop being a stupid old sod and accept that this is not your fault and move on with your life?"

Chris looked ready to punch Marty to the floor, but his clenched fist relaxed and they embraced instead. When they broke Chris looked more his old self.

"Feel better?" Marty asked.

"A little. But if you ever hit me again I won't dig a hole, just leave you to the dogs."

"Fair enough." Marty led Chris away from the graves, letting two of the minister's aides fill them in later. They walked back to the tents together.

"I mean it. You'd have no teeth left," Chris continued.

"I get it. So you don't love me?"

"Not a bit."

"Good. I wanna live a long and happy life."

"In that case I love you more than life itself."

Marty broke away. "I'm going solo now. This is too much personal interaction for me."

Chris looked hurt until they both broke into fresh laughter, the pain subdued by the bond they shared.

Back at the tents Jake ignored the slumped form at the abandoned beer cart, going back to his own tent. Greg sat alone and lost. In front of his crowds, when all eyes were on him he froze. He'd thrown away his chance of winning, and worse, his own self image was shattered. He'd always been the guy who came running into danger to save the victims, at least the ones who could pay. Today he froze like a bird and watched as his own surprise managed to surprise him.

He knew Spencer's woman had been killed by an Allo. Stepped on was what he had heard. He also knew half of Ben was inside one. The carcasses were being butchered right now, and if they find his upper body it will be lowered into the earth with his legs. He knew today he had performed badly, but to his greater shock he wasn't concerned with that. The competition seemed pointless, even laughable. To think he was willing to wish death upon his competitors, tricking and scheming ways to make them fail. What kind of man does that?

Spencer and his kid walked past laughing. The sound grated, but Greg let it. Joy was something he doubted he would ever know. Soon, before the sun set, they would be called to find who won. Greg was happy to walk away and not look back. He ignored Spencer, who was waving a greeting, instead Greg looked at the dirt below his feet, the dirt that covered his dreams, and would soon be covering his companion.

He had known Ben for a long time, but never really called him a friend. He was at best an assistant, at worst a student to teach and condition. Now there was only Jake left. At the thought Greg lifted his head. Jake was still here, and he would need firm but gentle guidance. This was not the time to fall apart, but it was time they regrouped and came back stronger. This was a lesson, not a test. He could run away or learn. Greg chose to learn. He went after Jake, his future clearer in his mind.

Chapter 36

All four men stood together before the city gates as the mayor impatiently nudged the announcer. Greg had seen Spencer talking to the man before they began, who looked more than a little surprised. Jake had calmed down a lot, especially when the butchers had found Ben's body in a stomach so it could be buried with his legs. The knowledge Ben was complete more or less had a soothing effect on Jake's rage. Now they stood together, the same as Spencer and his boy did.

"Gentlemen, Hunters of the highest calibre," the announcer said. "You have excelled in the arena, and proven to be skilled above all others. However, there can only be one winner. In spite of the skill that Hunter Chris Spencer and Martin Fritz-Herbert showed in combating the monsters that appeared at the close of proceeding , it is the choice of this panel that Hunter Greg Numlok is the champion Hunter."

"That would be Greg Numlok and Jake Smith," Greg said, surprising everyone.

"Very well," the announcer said, irritated to be kept out any longer than he needed to be. "Hunter Greg Numlok and Jake Smith. You are hereby given permission to dwell in our great city, as a citizen and defender of the city and its citizens."

A scroll of strong paper was handed by the mayor to Greg, who bowed slightly, then passed it to Jake. The mayor shook Greg's hand, nodding to Jake, then left. The others followed. Greg hung back, waiting in the gateway. The massive wooden gates were nearly closed, the guards waiting for Greg and Jake to come inside.

"I have only one question," Greg asked Chris.

"I guess I know what it is but ask anyway."

"Why did you turn down this prize?"

Chris smiled. "Who says I did?"

"I know that after those things came in I had lost. I froze, and a good Hunter never freezes."

"We do sometimes, when we need to. I don't want to live in a city. That would be hell to me, being trapped inside those walls. For you, that's a dream. So you have your dream."

"What about you?" Greg asked.

Marty looked at Chris, who shrugged. "I already have my dream," Chris said.

Greg looked lost, then realisation dawned. He nodded, then held out a hand Chris shook it. Jake gave Marty a hug, then the city's newest residents went inside. The huge gates swung closed and the sound of the bars being placed inside was final.

"So we living outside again?" Marty asked.

"Looks like it. You wanna be in there?"

"Not really. Don't think they are my kind of people."

"What is your kind of people?"

Marty tapped the door, noting how solid the wood was. "There are no people that are my kind of people."

"Just like me," Chris said.

"Just like you."

They walked back to the car together. The sun was a fire on the horizon, the graves now two mounds in the field. They had to pack, repair the trailer, and get home so they could come out again before the rains and snows came.

"So we good?" Marty asked as they walked.

"We good. By the way."

"What?"

Chris paused. "I love you, man."

"Oh crap. I'm a dead man."

Chris punched him gently and they walked away laughing.

Greg followed the mayor with the train of officials behind them. They walked through the city with everyone stopping to stare. It was clean inside the walls, although the smell of the sea and curing fish hung in the sheltered areas. Greg also noticed the people here seemed much better dressed than he expected, wearing clothes of clean browns and greens. His eye was caught by several young ladies wearing white, most showing their figures in the gauzy fabric. He asked the mayor why some wore white to be told that officials wore white or grey, fishermen for brown and the workers wore green. The white clad ladies were girls reaching joining age. It seemed strange to wear clothes depending on your occupation but Greg wasn't going to complain about the girls.

They stopped at a large house not far from the gates. Here was a small courtyard with a toilet that drained into the river, a small kitchen and a storeroom. Upstairs was a single large bedroom with wooden cupboards for his clothes, a wash basin, and a small anteroom for his weapons.

"All offensive weapons must be kept here until you are required to work for us," the mayor explained. "This is where you will stay. You may visit the city, but please keep yourself here as much as possible."

"Be a bit boring here just the two of us," Greg said, looking around the room.

"That is not my concern," the mayor answered with open irritation. "You will be on instant readiness should you be needed."

"What about the rewards?" Jake asked, picking up a loaf of bread.

"There is a financial safehouse in the centre of the city. All valuables are stored there. Your reward for winning the contest, along with your payments are stored there."

"Weapons?" Greg asked, pacing the large room and patting the soft bed.

"There is an armourer who can repair your equipment supplied by the city for free. Your own weapons are at your own expense. I believe it is time you began training in the courtyard." The mayor made a move for the door.

"We start immediately," Greg said. "Immediately in a few days."

"Agreed. I'm in no rush to go anywhere."

"Me neither."

The mayor clicked his tongue in irritation and left.

"I can't believe Spencer gave up all this," Jake said, chewing on more bread.

"Yeah, me too," Greg replied, distracted. He looked at the ceiling, then stood. Waving Jake back he headed down to the courtyard, his cart was already there, having been checked by the guards and then pulled in by a mule. Greg ignored the cart, instead he tried to find his way back to the gate. He found it after some trouble and was allowed outside. He found the tent village was almost gone, just one left near where the beer cart had been. The sounds of metal banging told him Spencer was still there.

Greg hesitated by the tent flap, then went inside. In the open section Spencer's car thing was there, the bit he pulled along was behind but in pieces. Spencer was working on it with a mallet. He saw Greg and stopped.

"Can I help?" Chris asked.

"I need a word," Greg said, turning away before he got a response. Chris shrugged to Marty and followed, one hand on his pistol. Marty cocked his head in thought, then joined them. Outside the sun still beat down, but it seemed to be less enthusiastic about burning the earth as if feeling tenderness to the new bodies lying under the surface.

"Why?" Greg asked.

"Why what?"

Greg sighed then turned around slowly. He faced Chris and Marty with almost resigned amusement. "Did you know about the rewards for the winner?"

"A little bird told me," Chris said, seeing Piers walk out the gates. The guard saw Greg and turned around, heading back inside.

"So you knew of the food, the shelter, the Luxuries?"

"Luxuries?" Marty asked.

"I knew," Chris replied, waving Marty's unanswered question away.

"So I say again, why?" Greg said.

"Why what?"

"Why did you tell them you didn't want to win?"

Marty looked from Greg to Chris. "We didn't lose or give in," he said. "We just didn't do it fancy enough, did we, Chris?"

"He quit," Greg said.

"Like hell would we? This old fool never quits." Marty squared off to Greg, his winter built physique still smaller but more powerful than Greg's long built figure.

"He told the officials he didn't want to win."

Marty laughed. "Tell this fur covered idiot that's rubbish," he said to Chris.

"We quit, Marty," came the half satisfied smile. "We quit because the city life isn't for us."

"How do you know what was me? I only found out myself a few days ago."

"I don't know what *was* you, I only know what is you." Chris laid a hand on his shoulder. "Yeah, ok so the house and food would be nice, but living in a city, tied to their rules, their schedule? And having to work when we get told to?"

"Sounds like a job," Marty said.

"Exactly. We work for ourselves. Nobody else."

Marty nodded. "So you told them to let the dog win?"

"What dog?" Greg asked. Marty pointed at him and laughed. Chris laughed too.

"Pretty much," Chris said. "Flair here is now the new pet for the city, to be used as they seem fit. He's got a job, with a boss and a nice little wage for it."

"I'm nobody's pet," Greg protested.

"You are now. All those nasty jobs nobody in there wants to do, the dangerous ones. Those are your future now. I've seen it before in Laden. They have people who do all the things that can kill to save their own people. Congratulations."

Greg saw Chris extend a hand, but didn't shake it. Instead he turned on one heel and stormed away. Marty barked at him, making the man pause, shaking his anger off, before he went inside.

"We going free again?" Marty asked when Greg had gone.

"We're free again. Too much out there for us to do without being stuck in some city."

"No rips in our clothes, yeah?"

"No rips. I'd rather die a hungry free man, than be a happy slave." Chris led Marty back to the car.

"So all we have to do is fix the trailer, gather our kit and go home?"

"Yeah. Plenty of time for you to tell me what is going on with you."

Marty broke free. "Not yet. I'm not ready yet. I need to know how to say what I have to say."

Looking carefully at the younger man Chris read his eyes. "Ok," he said eventually. "Whenever you're ready."

"Be more like when you are ready."

"That too." Chris read the sky, then got a drink of water from the bucket inside the tent.

Piers popped his head inside the inner tent.

"Quick word?" he asked.

"Anything for you," Chris said, offering the metal cup full of water.

"No, thanks. I just wanted to say thanks again." Piers squatted down beside the unlit stove.

"For what?"

"Firstly for helping me at Laden. Secondly for not making a drama here, and finally for not winning."

"Well the first was nothing, the second was because we did nothing, and the third makes no sense." Chris sat on the floor and rubbed a knee.

"Old wounds?" Piers asked.

"Old age. What about us not winning?"

"I heard you told them to let Greg win. I'm glad. The idea of you guys trapped in a city worries me."

"You think we'd cause trouble?" Marty asked, taking the cup from Chris.

"Partly. But mostly because you guys are the best, and you are the best because you keep sharp. A blade goes dull when you use it too much, but then you sharpen it. Leave it alone for a while and it loses it's edge." Piers finally accepted the cup from Marty. "You guys keep sharp."

"We will," Chris said. "When you going back to Laden?"

"A couple of days. There's a convoy coming soon with seed for the factories. Once they get here we'll be riding back with the full tankers of fuel and oil."

"Well, good luck. Hope we see you before we leave." Chris stood and waited for Piers. They shook hands and the guard left.

"We finishing this trailer then?" Marty asked. Chris nodded and they set to work with the tools again.

Chapter 37

Two days later, when Piers' convoy was arriving, Chris and Marty checked the trailer, ready to leave. The sun was barely up and it felt chilly for once, a sign the season was passing. Nobody from the city came out to see them leave, and none had visited since Piers left. Marty looked at the yellow patches of ground where the tents had been, the worn space for the beer cart, and the tree line that hid the arena.

"Face like that I'll use you as a horse," Chris said.

"You what?"

"I said, never mind. Doesn't matter. You ready?"

"As I'll ever be." Marty slid into his seat, giving the city one last look, the high walls towering over them. He heard a shout and a small figure above waved. It was Piers. He shouted something and dropped a bundle of rags. Marty ran to get it. Inside was some bread and cheese, and a note.

"Nice to see you again, old friends. Keep in touch," Marty read aloud, following the lines with his finger.

"We will," Chris said. He started the old diesel engine and waited for it to shake itself into a smooth rhythm. Once warmed up they drove on, Marty half turning to watch the city fall behind. Piers still waved from the top of the walls and Marty waved back until he couldn't see the man anymore, just the patched wall and the glint of water inside as they climbed the hill. Over the summit the ground swallowed the settlement and the two bodies that lay nearby.

They drove in silence, Chris holding his tongue. Marty was random when it came to moods, and after finding out about his past he was even more so. He could easily go from almost elated to seriously depressed instantly. The slightest thing could change his temperament severely so he kept silent, hoping Marty would find his own voice soon enough.

As a larger village passed by Marty finally spoke.

"We near home?" he asked.

"Not yet. Be near dark by the time we get there."

Marty looked at the sky. "Pull over."

"You see something?"

"I need to say something."

Chris shot him a puzzled look, but the ground here was open and with a village nearby they should be fairly safe. He stopped the car and took his rifle. They checked the area around them, then Chris stood on the flat bonnet while Marty sat on the side, his long legs dangling.

"What you need to say then?" Chris asked.

"Give me a minute."

Chris didn't like being still too long but he also wanted Marty to get this off his chest. So he waited and watched. The voice that came after an eternity was like the wind, soft and secretive.

"I found out who I was," Marty breathed. "When I lived over the water I was a seaman, like the fishermen. Only my family didn't fish for fish. We fished for people. Apparently my father was the best slave trader ever. We had a ship, not a boat. It was massive apparently. That's where I lived, where I was born. We'd go ashore somewhere and find a village. Then we'd kill the old and take everyone else. Each person was given a price then locked below. Back in the big cities over there you get a good price for strong men and pretty women so I used to be the one to sort them. The men you could tell by looking at them. The women you had to try them.

"I used to do things to them, horrible things. If they tried to fight me they didn't fight for long. If they didn't satisfy I killed them." His voice cracked, anger and grief mixing into a frustration that had been eating him inside all his life. "I used to feed the bodies of the dead to the living because it amused me. I would beat the children of parents until they did what I told them to. I tore families apart. I was young, but I had size and I used it to do what I wanted, no matter who was hurt. Damn it, Chris. I'm a Raider."

Chris dropped off the car bonnet and walked away a few paces. He lowered the rifle and rubbed his face with his free hand.

"How can I live with what I am?" Marty asked. He looked up to see the rifle pointing at him.

"What you were, or what you are?" Chris asked.

"What you asking?" Marty didn't blink at the muzzle facing him.

"Are you still a Raider, or are you now a Hunter?"

"What kind of question is that? I was a Raider, and that made me a good Hunter. I did all the things I hate."

"Exactly. You did all the things you hate. You don't do them now. So, I'll ask you again. Are you a Raider or a Hunter."

"I want to be a Hunter. I want to make up for all the evil I've done."

Chris looked down the sights at Marty. After an age he lowered the rifle.

"You already have. Accepting your guilt and wanting to repay the damage makes you a man, not one of those monsters."

Marty shook his head. "That's not the worst of it."

"What could be worse?"

A deep breath came before the click. Marty took his pistol and threw it to Chris. "You may want to use that when I tell you about this next bit."

"Nothing would make me kill you if you don't want to be a Raider."

"This will."

Chris bit his lip. "Then tell me and we'll see."

"When we were blown over here by a big storm we started raiding for supplies inland. We attacked villages. We were the only Raider party in this area. That means we hit all the villages, including yours. I can't prove it, or not, but the way you described the attack, and the banner they used, it was ours, our ship's flag. That memory is far too clear to be wrong. It was us who killed your family. That you found me the next year sounds about right. It was me. I don't expect forgiveness, but I am sorry, so sorry."

Chris turned away, fist clenched. The memory of the death of his wife and child ran through his mind's eye. The banner the Raiders had used to identify clans. He'd never found that band, and no wonder if they lived on the sea. His village wasn't near the coast, but if the nearer villages had been hit they would be found eventually. Pain and grief flared powerfully through his body, making him pant.

Behind him Marty sobbed on the car. He knew that the loss of his family, his home had forced Chris to run. He'd found the bunker and the next cycle he'd found Marty lost and confused. He'd hated Raiders and now to find he was one was like finding his hands were not his own. He loathed himself and wanted only to forget again.

"Did you kill them?" Chris asked.

"I don't know. I remember our banner, *their* banner. It was the same one you described. I can't remember villages, or attacks."

"How did you end up in the wild when I found you?" His voice was tense, but Chris was trying to work out everything before he made a decision.

"One village I was injured in the attack. They helped me back, but apparently I wandered off one night. They looked but couldn't find me. My parents thought I was dead so they left. A few days later the ship was in a storm. It sank with everyone onboard, including the slaves. One of the crew made it to shore. He became a fisherman in that city. When he saw me he knew who I was. I worked on their boat for a while until he was sure it was me. Then he explained my past. I remember now, but I'd do anything to forget again."

Chris still faced away, looking at the village without seeing it. His mind raced like clouds on a windy day. His whole world was turned over, spilling memories and feelings like water. Marty was saying something about apologising again, but the words were dull and hollow. Instead Chris walked away. His anger and the loaded rifle in his hands were too dangerous a combination. Marty whistled.

"I understand," he said. "Go. Leave me here. I can move into the village there. Part of the reason I asked you to stop here. Leave me and never look back." Marty dropped off the wing of the car and took off his equipment belt, laying it on the bonnet. He didn't look at Chris but instead turned and walked towards the village. Chris took the belt and the pistol from the ground and got into the car. He started the engine and drove away. Marty heard the sound and kept walking, his vision blurred by tears. His old life was over. He didn't know how to farm, or rear animals, but he could learn. He had to learn. The car headed away, kicking up dust from the parched ground. The village walls grew as Marty walked, the mud and dirt patched like the big cities, beige instead of grey. He tried to think of how he would introduce himself but all he could think of was the pain on Chris' face when he found out who killed his family.

The gate was on the other side of the village so Marty had to walk around. The sun burnt the back of his neck but that was the least of his troubles. Finding the heavy gate he was surprised it was open. Inside the village elder was waiting with Chris.

"You really are a slow walker," Chris said, leaning on the side of the car.

"What the hell?" Marty asked.

Chris shook hands with the elder, then stood facing Marty. "We all do stupid stuff in our past. I never judge someone on who they were, only who they are now. You aren't that man anymore. You weren't since I met you. You've done some evil things, things that Parks would be impressed with. But that doesn't make you evil. Nor does it make you Parks. You're Marty, and that's a guy I can travel with."

Marty broke into fresh tears as they embraced. He held tight, trembling.

"Enough," Chris said. "We're professionals. We have to look it. These guys need our help." He pulled Marty off, prising the man's arms away. "They have a wildlife issue. We stay here tonight."

Marty nodded and hesitantly got into the car. Chris slid in beside him and they drove towards the back of the village.

"It will take time," Chris said, "but one day I will fully trust you again. I trust you enough to work with you, and that's a start."

"That's all I need, a start."

"You got it. Let's get to work."

They set up camp behind a store hut. Some young ladies came over, impressed with Marty. Chris watched but the young man waved them away. Usually he'd dive in with them. Maybe he was changing, but this was for the better.

Chapter 38

Greg lay on the bed. From the other side of the room Jake was snoring like a pig among a morning bird chorus. They had been in bed for three days. Outside in the small courtyard some metal bars had been made for them to use for training, and a grinding wheel to sharpen blades with. Neither men had seen them, and anyone who came to visit was told to leave in a manner dependent on how the request was made, and how often. So when the door knocker banged they shouted for the visitor to leave. The door opened anyway.

"Greeting, Hunters," said a man they didn't know. "I am your assistant to the mayor. He requests you rise as there is work for you to do."

"What kind of work?" Greg asked from his pillow.

"We have a problem in one of the small farms north of the city. Some wild animals have damaged crops and equipment."

"What do they look like?"

"We do not know. Nobody has seen the animals, only the damage left by them. Hurry please." The assistant left, leaving the door open. Greg looked at Jake, who shrugged then dropped his head back on his pillow.

"My idea exactly," Greg said, wriggling into his bed a little deeper.

"Hurry, please," the assistant said from the doorway.

"Later," Greg murmured.

"You are in the employ of the city, and therefore you will serve the city. Now please rise and get ready." The assistant strode in and clapped his hands. Three large men came in and stood by the doorway looking menacing.

"Hey!" Greg moaned. Jake rolled over and pulled a heavy blanket over himself.

"The city will not pay you to sit around when there is work to be done. You will rise immediately or I shall have to ask these guards to get you up." The assistant left, the threat hanging in the air like a vulture.

"I'm beginning to see where Spencer was coming from," Greg said.

"Yeah. Me too," replied Jake, rolling out from under his blanket.

"Still, could be worse. At least here we have food, women and a safe place to sleep. Just need to do a few jobs. No worse than it was outside."

"Better in fact."

Greg nodded. "Much. Come on. Let's solve this little problem."

"Agreed. The sooner we solve it the sooner we can come back to our warm beds."

Downstairs the assistant looked unimpressed.

"I see you finally got out of bed," he said.

"We did. Where's this problem?" Greg asked, checking his blades while Jake used the wheel to sharpen a knife.

"North of the city, as I had already said. Hurry. There could be more damage and maybe even a loss of life."

"Calm yourself. We need time to check our weapons."

"If you spent less time in bed you'd have more time to have your equipment ready." The assistant frowned and left. Outside four city guards followed him.

"Nice guy," Jake said from the wheel.

"Bet we could be good friends in the future."

"If you got him drunk maybe."

Greg laughed and lifted some of the metal bars, appreciating the weight and the way it made his arms look bigger. Looking over his blades he used some of the lamp oil the city refined to oil his best blades, then waved Jake to join him. Using the sun they headed north towards their first job as Hunters for the city.

Chris and Marty worked their way north towards the bunker. With most of the Hunters at the trials there was a lot of threats roaming around unchecked. Raiders had attacked one village, killing all the people who lived there and a Hunter they had hired to protect them. Chris saw the smoke from the Raiders' attack and steered the car towards the high mud walls. They found three men by the broken gates. They cried over the loss of their families. They had been out finding their few animals when the attack came.

"We'll find them," Chris promised one red eyed man. He knew they didn't stand a chance over the coming cold. They had food and shelter to support a whole village for winter, even after the raiders had taken all they could. But left alone the three men would grow old and die unless they could find another village to live in.

"I'll bring you their heads," Marty added, ignoring the stern look from Chris.

"Please, we thank you," the man said, smiling for the first time all day.

Chris walked away, looking for a trail the Raiders will have left behind. Marty hung back, but stopped by the car before joining Chris. He'd filled his pockets and the pouches in his equipment belt with ammunition and water. Watching the low, yellow grass he let Chris search.

Staring intently at the ground as if asking it for directions Chris searched for the trail. Raiders didn't do anything subtly. There would be blood, half eaten food and bits of the rotting furs they wore that would even lead a child after them. Chris found the trail without much effort and followed, rifle slung on his shoulder. He half jogged as he followed the footprints and debris in the baked dirt.

Near the village was a stand of a few trees. From there the sounds of moans and cheering could be heard. Chris didn't need to see them to know the raiders were there, and they had kept some of the women from the village for their pleasure. He squatted down near the trees, keeping out of sight. Idly drumming his fingers on his rifle stock Chris waved Marty down and thought. Finally he shrugged and knelt up. Waving Marty left Chris went right. They moved silently into the trees, easily seeing each other through the slender trunks. In the middle was a dried up pond and there lay fifteen Raiders. Three were holding down a woman while another raped her. Two more women lay nearby, crying softly.

With a hand gesture Chris stopped Marty and they knelt in unison. Raising his rifle Chris looked down the iron sights and gently eased the safety catch off. It stuck, then clicked loudly. The Raiders still shouted loudly but one looked up. He looked puzzled as the rifle round went through his forehead. The others' stopped and watched as the body slowly sank. By the time they realised what was happening two men burst from the scruffy bushes that surrounded the trees. They used sticks but they spat fire and more fell. The last few alive knew it was hopeless and ran.

Chris caught one and threw him to the floor. He looked up to see Marty facing the other three who survived. They held out their hands pleading with him. With one boot on the throat of his Raider Chris watched carefully. Marty held his rifle steady, but he didn't fire. One of the men crawled forwards on his hand and knees, rambling about how he was sorry and didn't want to be a Raider anymore. The other two watched in disgust. Marty didn't move.

Chris watched, but kept silent. He saw the man under his foot move, saw the flash of a blade, and he reversed his rifle and slammed the butt on the raider's head and the blade fell from his hand. Marty still watched the man as he crawled towards him.

"I'm sorry," the Raider pleaded. "I no mean to hurt, to kill. I must or I lose home, lose family." The man kept up his rambling, crying and clawing the ground. As he drew close to Marty he knelt up. The blade came from nowhere, slicing the afternoon air and reflecting the sunlight. Marty leant sideways, letting the blade flicker past him, then pressed the muzzle into the man's temple. He fired, destroying the face that still cried. The other two dropped their concealed blades as they drew them, turning to run. Marty calmly fired two shots and both men fell.

"I didn't know if you were actually going to fire then," Chris said.

"Why didn't you?" Marty asked, looking at the unconscious man on the floor.

"To see what you did. I always kill these things. You *were* one. So I needed to know where your loyalty lies."

"With you."

"I see that now."

Marty kicked the unconscious raider on the floor gently, the man moaning. "Thought you killed them all."

"I'm saving this one."

"Why?"

Chris smiled. "Look closer."

Marty knelt down beside the man. Even with the heat of the sun on his back he shivered when he saw the patch. He looked up at Chris who nodded.

"This is one of yours. Thought you might wanna talk to him."

"Why would I talk to that?" Marty asked, standing up.

"To find out more of your past."

Marty looked from the Raider to Chris. He drew his pistol and shot the man in one fluid motion. Checking the breech of the pistol Marty slid it back into his belt holster. "I have no past," he said and walked back to the car. Chris smiled slightly as he watched his friend walk away. He had grown a lot this cycle, and not just physically. Leaving the bodies to the animals he followed Marty back to the village. They helped the women who survived, much to Marty's confusion.

"You don't normally save the victims," he hissed to Chris as they each carried a woman back, the third was already dead.

"I know, but these have a home to go to, and men to care for them. That village will die without them," Chris whispered back.

They laid the women down by the surviving men and helped them treat their wounds both mental and physical. Once the villagers were safe Chris and Marty repaired the gates and moved the Land Rover inside. Keeping watch all night they took turns to sleep. In the early morning the villagers slept on so the Hunters silently left, keeping away from the bodies of the Raiders.

"Home time?" Marty asked as the sun rose beside them.

"Yeah, home time. Been too long and we need to restock before we go out again. Plenty of sowing season left."

"Sounds good to me. I need more time on those weights."

"You hoping to look like Greg?" Chris teased.

"Yeah, but with brains as well."

"Who says you have brains?"

"Me," Marty replied with a smug smile.

"I don't think that's a reliable opinion."

They drove in silence, heading into the big forest that hid the bunker at it's heart. Marty kept watch on the thick trees while Chris picked the best route in, making sure they didn't get stuck. When the familiar hill the bunker lay in peeked through the trees Marty sighed in relief. The hiss of surprise from Chris robbed him of any feeling of peace.

The big door to the bunker lay open. Traps laid by Chris were either destroyed or ripped from the ground and scattered. The lights were out, but debris and dirt told them more than enough. Stopping the car by the edge of the clearing Chris waved Marty to keep watch while he went inside.

The hanger was empty. All the containers, all the vehicles, all the weapons were gone. Only the massive metal birds and trucks that rolled on long tracks were left. The weapons' locker had been forced open, all the ammunition inside was gone. The fuel tanks were dry and some had been poured into the water tanks, fouling the tanks and the water inside. The overhead lights had been smashed and even the training room was a mess of bent metal and broken glass. Walking around in a daze Chris tried to work out who could have done this when he saw a piece of paper pinned to a wall by one of their own knives.

'Ha ha. Parks'.

Chris' howl of rage brought Marty running inside, only to see Chris kneeling on the floor, reading the note again and breathing heavily.

"What the hell?" Marty asked, looking around.

"That's exactly where he is going," Chris said. Without saying anything he stood and walked out. Marty followed, looking back over his shoulder as he walked just in case anyone was still inside.

"What the hell we doing then?" Marty asked when they were back at the car.

"I don't know about you, but that little bugger is getting the worst kicking of his life."

"With what?"

Chris smiled in a way that scared Marty. "He will see, and he will not want to believe it."

Chapter 39

They fixed the metal door so they could secure the bunker first. Then Marty made a full check on what was left. It was bleak. He recited the list to a numb looking Chris, afraid of the man's reactions.

"So they took all the weapons, cars and equipment. Anything left they smashed. The metal birds are fine, they left those alone. Also the metal tank car things were ignored. Too hard to damage I suppose. All the fuel is gone save some they pumped into the water tanks. They also crapped in there so the water is definitely undrinkable. The library, barracks and training rooms are either smashed or gone, and they took all the food. Basically they cleaned us out."

"I noticed," Chris said in a lifeless tone.

"How the hell could they do it in the short time we were gone?"

Chris stood and walked casually to a wall. He looked at it, then punched it hard. Massaging his fist he turned back to Marty.

"I should have guessed it," he said, rubbing his hand. "I should have seen it. Parks knew from Ryder roughly where we were hiding when we found him. All he had to do was search for this place. Then he came over while we were away at that damn Trial and helped himself."

"But how could he know we would be at the Trials?" Marty asked. "We weren't going originally."

"True, but I bet he had someone watching here once they found it. Someone good."

"A Hunter?"

"Probably. He wanted to take all our stuff the way I took his."

Marty smiled and pointed at the car. "He didn't find that. It's about the only thing he didn't get."

"Well, I guess that's something." Chris walked over to the Land Rover, looking lost and small in the massive empty space.

"Now we know who, what will we do about it?" Marty asked.

Chris looked over the car. Parks took all the weapons, fuel cans and food from the lockers. Marty checked the door over then helped take stock. Once everything was laid out on the hard floor it looked pitiful.

"Not very much left, is there?" Chris said, mostly to himself.

"We can't even get to Parks' city with this," Marty agreed, kicking a fuel can with one boot.

"We don't need to." Chris left a confused Marty by the car and headed into the back of the bunker. He returned with a metal box.

"You fancy helping an old man?" he asked Marty. "There are three more out back."

Marty ran past Chris and saw a section of the wall had been prised open, showing ammunition boxes and packs of food.

"When did you hide this?" Marty asked.

"At the start, when I first found this place. I was learning woodwork and I thought I could put a partition wall in. It was going to be a room for me and any woman I could find to join with, but in the end it made more sense to be a stash instead. I put a lot of ammo and food in here."

"That helps, but did you hide fuel in there?"

Chris smiled, back to his old self. "I didn't need to." He led Marty to the storage tanks. Here were four large underground tanks, each easily twenty feet across and much more down. The two right hand ones were water, the left two were fuel. Chris walked around the domed tank tops and punched the wall behind them. His fist went easily through the ply board and with some effort he made a hole big enough to squeeze through. There were more tanks inside.

"That's quite impressive," Marty said, clapping slowly.

"I pumped most of the fuel and water into the back tanks. That way we only had enough to keep us going. Means if we have a damaged tank we don't lose all our fuel or water."

"I think we will survive for now, but what about Parks? He now has enough equipment to take on the world."

"And win," Chris added grimly. "I think it best that we vanish."

"You mean run away?" Marty looked shocked at the suggestion.

"Never run away, just vanish. If he thinks we're dead and gone then it's easier to react. Ghosts can go anywhere."

"I like this plan. Not the dead part, but I could be a ghost for a while."

Chris began pumping fuel into one of the empty tanks. "We can give old Parks the rest of this cycle until harvesting to dig himself a big enough hole, then we go take back everything."

"How can we go up against an army of men armed the same as us?"

"We don't." Chris turned away from the pumps.

Marty looked lost and followed Chris when he walked out. "If we don't then who will?"

Chris stopped and slapped Marty on the shoulder. "We get our own army."

"With what?"

Chris went back to the shattered barrack rooms. With some effort he found the wooden panel hidden under the rubber floor covering. Heaving it away he pulled out a familiar wooden box. Opening it he took out a roll of paper.

"With this," Chris said, a childlike smile on his face. He waved the paper at Marty until he understood. Both laughing they sat in the remains of their home and planned their return, and their revenge.

Firstly I would like to thank you for getting to the end of this, my sixth book. It's hard to believe sometimes that this series is half of my work. It nearly didn't even happen. The first was just a practice for me but proved so popular it never really stopped. As I write this the fourth in the Chris Spencer series is beside my writing laptop, edited but not yet past the second draft. So for now at least the adventures of Chris and Marty will continue. I'm happy about that as I feel real affection towards these two. They are old friends to me, and by now I hope you feel the same.

James

30/11/21

Printed in Great Britain
by Amazon

75355223R00190